She was gazing drowsily into the fire when Zander's hand softly stroked her cheek.

She smiled dreamily and turned her face up to his, giving a sigh of pleasure as his mouth brushed hers.

Her lips parted beneath the light pressure of his, and when he deepened the kiss her arms went around his neck. Her whole body melting, she kissed him back.

Then, suddenly scared by her own reaction to that kiss, she drew back, demanded raggedly, 'Why did you do that? You had no right to kiss me. Don't ever do it again. I hated it!'

As soon as the words were out she knew she'd made a bad mistake.

She sat still as any statue as his hands moved to cup her chin and tilt her head back, so that she found herself looking up into his handsome face, intriguingly inverted.

'So tell me,' he said silkily, 'if my kiss is such anathema to you, why did you kiss me back?'

Lee Wilkinson lives with her husband in a three-hundred-year-old stone cottage in a Derbyshire village, which most winters gets cut off by snow. They both enjoy travelling, and recently, joining forces with their daughter and son-in-law, spent a year going round the world 'on a shoestring' while their son looked after Kelly, their much loved German shepherd dog. Her hobbies are reading and gardening, and holding impromptu barbecues for her long-suffering family and friends.

Recent titles by the same author:

CLAIMING HIS WEDDING NIGHT
CAPTIVE IN THE MILLIONAIRE'S CASTLE
THE BOSS'S FORBIDDEN SECRETARY
MISTRESS AGAINST HER WILL

Did you know these are also available as eBooks?
Visit www.millsandboon.co.uk

RUNNING
FROM THE STORM

BY
LEE WILKINSON

MILLS & BOON

First published in Great Britain 2012
by Mills & Boon, an imprint of Harlequin (UK) Limited.
Harlequin (UK) Limited, Eton House, 18-24 Paradise Road,
Richmond, Surrey TW9 1SR

© Lee Wilkinson 2012

ISBN: 978 0 263 89043 3

Harlequin (UK) policy is to use papers that are natural, renewable and recyclable products and made from wood grown in sustainable forests. The logging and manufacturing process conform to the legal environmental regulations of the country of origin.

Printed and bound in Spain
by Blackprint CPI, Barcelona

RUNNING
FROM THE STORM

To Ned

CHAPTER ONE

THE twelfth-century, lichen-covered church was filled with the fragrance of roses and lilies and the strains of Mendelssohn's traditional and well-loved *Here Comes The Bride*.

Bright sunshine slanted through the stained-glass windows and, as the trees in the churchyard moved in the breeze, made changing kaleidoscope patterns across the backs of the polished pews and the grey stone slabs of the floor.

Nothing seemed quite real as Caris walked slowly up the aisle on the arm of her Uncle David. Her father, still angry with her, had refused to give her away.

A man, presumably the best man, was waiting by the chancel steps. He had his back to her and she couldn't see his face.

There was no sign of her groom.

On both sides of the aisle the congregation turned their heads to look and smile at her as she passed in a froth of white tulle that, even then, she knew was all wrong for her.

She did her best to smile back, but her face felt set and stiff, as though it was made from wax, and she couldn't.

As she reached the chancel steps she was aware that her bridegroom had joined her and was standing by her side. She didn't look at him.

The elderly priest stepped forward, gathered the congregation's attention with a glance and began with the traditional words, 'Dearly beloved, we are gathered here together...'

While the wedding service solemnly progressed, Caris stared straight ahead and asked herself what she was doing here.

When they reached the point where she and her bridegroom needed to make their vows and she still refused to look at him, he took her upper arms and turned her to face him.

His green eyes were cool, commanding; his blond, well-shaped head had that slightly arrogant tilt she knew so well.

'Say it, Caris.'

But she couldn't. This was all wrong! She couldn't, *wouldn't*, marry Zander!

Dropping the bouquet of pale-pink roses she carried, she turned and, gathering up her full skirts, fled down the aisle between the rows of gaping guests, tears pouring down her cheeks.

She could hear him calling after her, 'Don't go, Caris... Don't go...'

But she *had* to. No matter how much she loved him, she wouldn't marry a man who didn't love her, who could well suspect that he had been trapped into marriage.

Gasping for breath, sobs rising in her throat, she reached the gloomy inner porch of the church and flung open the heavy door.

Stumbling through into the outer porch, she was met by bright sunshine and a brisk breeze that blew the folds of the fine silken-net veil over her face.

The dreamer was endeavouring to tear off the suffocating veil when she awoke and, sitting bolt upright, found she was in her own bed, the uncertain light of a rainy, late-spring morning filtering in.

Even so, it was a few seconds before the panic subsided and the sight of her familiar room, with its pastel walls and pretty, flowered curtains, steadied her a little.

Somewhere nearby a car door slammed and she could hear

the unmistakable sounds of the quiet, tree-lined street coming alive—Billy Leyton's motorbike being kicked into life, the shush of tyres on the wet road, next door's dog barking.

Right on cue, the bedside alarm-clock announced with a loud jingle that it was seven-thirty.

'It was a dream,' Caris said aloud as she brushed a hand over her wet cheeks and reached to switch off the alarm. 'Just a dream.'

But a haunting, reoccurring dream that had disturbed her sleep and, like some earthquake, shaken her world, causing the ground beneath her feet to open into a gaping chasm.

Since coming to England almost three years ago, she had fought hard to push all thoughts of Zander and the past out of her mind, and over the last six months she had started to believe she was succeeding.

Despite the gloomy economic climate, the estate agency she ran kept her so busy that, immersed in work, she could sometimes go for days on end without thinking of him, days on end without picturing his face.

In consequence she had gradually gained some kind of shaky equilibrium. She was able, at last, to look back and put their relationship into perspective.

It hadn't been all bad.

Though it had ended in tears and heartache, for a while she had enjoyed the kind of happiness that she had never known existed.

And hadn't it been said repeatedly that it was better to have loved and lost than never to have loved at all?

Pleased that she was able to think that way, she had congratulated herself on her newly found emotional stability.

Now, all because of a dream, that had been swept away. She was once again off-balance and Zander was back in her head, his handsome, strong-boned face clear in her mind's eye.

All at once she felt cold and bereft. Churned up and desolate. All the old bitterness back.

But she wouldn't let a dream throw her into emotional chaos again. She was no longer the vulnerable, inexperienced, round peg in a square hole she had been when they had first met.

The painful three years she had just lived through had made a great deal of difference. Now, to all intents and purposes, she was a self-possessed, successful businesswoman in her own right.

If the assurance—the air of confidence, the polish—was only a veneer, these days she didn't allow anyone to get close enough to even scratch the surface, so who was to know?

To outsiders, she was what she appeared to be.

Partly reassured by this restored vision of a calm, secure, well-ordered life, Caris made her way to the bathroom to brush her teeth and shower.

When she was dried and dressed for the day—in a grey, lightweight business suit, discreetly made-up, her long dark hair taken up into a knot, small gold studs in her ears—she went through to the kitchen to make herself some toast and coffee.

It was the Saturday morning of a bank holiday weekend, a busy, working Saturday as far as Caris was concerned, in spite of the weather.

After a cold, wet spring and almost a week of heavy and prolonged rain, everyone had been hoping that, with the prospect of a warm front moving in, the bank holiday would stay dry.

But it was raining yet again, and the latest forecast had been for continuing heavy rain and severe thunderstorms.

In spite of the inclement weather and the continuing recession, Carlton Lees, the estate agency Caris now owned, was doing quite well.

After the death of her aunt, finding it almost impossible to run the agency single-handed, she had taken on a local girl, a cheerful eighteen-year-old named Julie Dawson.

Julie, who did the secretarial work and held the fort while Caris was out with clients, had proved to be an absolute godsend.

Sensible and mature for her years, when sales had started to pick up she had been quite willing to come in early and work late whenever it had proved to be necessary.

Properties in and around the quiet market town of Spitewinter, though moving relatively slowly, were at least moving, and just at present there was no lack of interested clients.

This was due partly to the only other estate agent in town closing down, and partly to the fact that several of the more sought-after properties had recently come on to the market.

The most notable of these was a small manor house dating from the fifteen-hundreds. It had been owned by a famous writer who, at ninety-eight, had recently died and left it to a distant cousin.

The cousin, who lived in Australia, had no desire to keep it. Wanting a speedy sale so he could buy his own ranch, he had put Gracedieu onto the market, causing a buzz of excitement and interest in the property world.

An article about the sale—lavishly accompanied by pictures of the house, estate and the 'sole agent, Miss Caris Belmont'—had appeared in one of the most prestigious magazines:

Gracedieu, a unique example of a small, sixteenth-century manor house, is an absolute gem. It stands in its own delightful estate which is complete with an old water-mill and a hamlet of picturesque, period cottages, especially built in the late seventeen-hundreds to house the estate workers…

This coverage had caused even more interest and, despite the astronomical asking price and the fact that it had been somewhat neglected by its previous owner, there were several potential buyers waiting to view the place.

The first of these had an appointment for that afternoon, and Caris knew her attention should be focused on getting a quick sale at the asking price.

But, though she tried her hardest to banish all thoughts of Zander, she found it impossible to get him out of her mind.

The Old Vicarage, bequeathed to her by her aunt, along with what had then been a struggling estate agency, all at once seemed too big and too empty, with nothing but regrets and ghosts from the past to keep her company.

Impatient with herself, anxious to get away, she jumped to her feet, grabbed her bag and mac and headed for the door.

Beaded with raindrops, her modest car was waiting on the driveway, and in a moment or two she had left the house behind and, with wipers clicking rhythmically, was heading into town.

Passing the library, she joined the light stream of traffic flowing through Spitewinter's High Street and across the old humpbacked bridge that spanned the willow-hung river, brown and swollen now because of all the recent rain.

When she reached Carlton Lees, which was at the end of a row of Dickensian shops situated in a wide, cobbled street by the river, she parked in her usual spot beneath the trees and ran to let herself in, her mac around her shoulders.

Julie hadn't yet arrived, and everywhere was quiet. After attending to the messages and emails, Caris found her client for that morning had been forced to cancel and had requested an appointment for the following week.

That dealt with, she tried to concentrate on the routine work, but tenuous threads of the dream still clung, sticky and inescapable as a spider's web, and in spite of all her efforts she found her thoughts going back three years.

Back to when her home had been in Upstate New York, and she had joined Belmont and Belmont, her father's well-respected law firm in Albany. It was there she had first met and fallen in love with Zander...

She had been sitting behind her desk one Friday evening, checking some legal documents before she went home, when her father had looked in to wish her a good vacation. 'You've earned it,' he'd added.

Austin Belmont, a clever, not to say brilliant lawyer, was a cold, unapproachable, irascible man who rarely handed out praise.

For as long as she could remember she had done her best to please him—with scant success. Now, his spoken approval left her open-mouthed and gasping.

Some half an hour later, she had just filed away the documents she'd been working on, and was about to go home, when the internal phone had rung.

'I'm sorry to bother you, Miss Belmont...' The firm's usually unflappable secretary sounded a little flustered. 'But I have a Mr Devereux here. I wonder if you could possibly see him?'

Devereux... The name rang a bell, though Caris couldn't immediately think why. 'Does he have an appointment?'

'He was supposed to see Mr David, but I'm afraid there's been a mix-up. We have the wrong date down, and both Mr Austin and Mr David have already left. I was on the point of leaving myself.'

Knowing Kate Bradshaw would need to pick up her daughter from the child minder, Caris said quickly, 'That's quite all right, Kate. If you would like to show Mr Devereux through before you go, I'll do what I can to help him.'

She heard a slight but unmistakable sigh of relief before the receiver was replaced, and guessed that their disgruntled client had been giving the poor woman a hard time.

A moment later there was a tap at the door and he was ushered in.

For some reason Caris had pictured him as being short and portly with grey, thinning hair and jowls, wearing a stuffy suit and tie.

The man who strode in, however, was attractive and self-assured, and carried with him an aura of power and authority.

He was somewhere in the region of twenty-seven or twenty-eight, she judged, blond and broad-shouldered, well over six-feet tall, dressed in smart casuals and looking anything but stuffy.

Beneath the thick, sun-streaked hair his handsome face was lean and tanned, with strong, clear-cut features and long, heavy-lidded eyes beneath curved brows several shades darker than his hair. His mouth, at first glance austere, held a hint of passion that sent shivers running up and down her spine.

Rising to her feet, she held out her hand. 'I'm Caris Belmont, Mr Devereux.'

She was vexed to find that, instead of being composed and businesslike, her voice sounded very slightly breathless.

Taking her hand, he said formally, 'Miss Belmont.'

As those long fingers wrapped around hers she felt an electric tingle run up her arm, and thought a trifle dazedly that she had read about that kind of thing happening in romantic novels but had never quite believed it.

Pulling herself together, she said, 'I gather there's been some kind of mix-up over the date of your appointment?'

His green eyes cool, he said a shade brusquely, 'So I understand. Though I must point out that the mistake wasn't mine.'

'No. I do apologize.'

If she had hoped for some softening in his attitude, she was disappointed. Clearly he wasn't the kind of man who took kindly to being brought on a wild goose chase.

She resumed her seat and, indicating the black leather armchair in front of her desk, asked politely, 'Won't you sit down?'

When he made no move to follow her suggestion, she added, 'I may be able to help you.'

He studied her with great deliberation for a moment or two before raising a well-marked brow and asking, 'In what way?'

Annoyed by the cool mockery, she said stiffly, 'I *am* a qualified lawyer.'

His manner holding a faint but unmistakable touch of incredulity, he drawled, 'Really?'

Her soft mouth tightened. How could she ever have thought him attractive? she wondered furiously. The man was so arrogant!

'Yes, really,' she said frigidly.

'How old are you, Miss Belmont? Let's see, you must be all of twenty-two—twenty-three at the most?'

Caris bit her lip. He had expected to see one of the senior partners and clearly he thought he was being fobbed off with an inexperienced junior.

Which in a way he was, honesty made her admit.

'I can't see that my age matters.'

'Then suppose I phrase that question differently. Have you had any actual experience?'

'Certainly... Lots,' she added recklessly.

'*Lots?* My! You must be older than you look. So exactly how long have you been with the practice?'

'Almost a year.' She tried not to sound defensive.

'That long!'

She gritted her teeth.

'And what exactly is your position here?'

She was pleased to be able to say, 'I've just been offered a partnership.'

The gleam in his eye told her that he knew quite well she had deliberately left out the word 'junior'.

'Tell me, Miss Belmont, what is the relationship between yourself and the senior partners? As the surname is the same, I take it there *is* one?'

Seething inwardly, because she already knew what he was getting at, she curbed her temper as best she could and said briefly, 'Austin Belmont is my father. David Belmont is my uncle.'

'So it's what you might call a nice, cosy little set-up.'

Her anger boiled over and she threw caution to the winds. 'Mr Devereux,' she said, her voice icy, 'I accept that you have a genuine reason for complaint, but I find your attitude insufferable.'

'And I find yours, shall we say, somewhat naive for a qualified lawyer.'

'In that case perhaps you would prefer to wait and talk to one of the senior partners?'

'I understood from your secretary that there is no one else available before Monday.'

'I'm afraid there isn't,' she confirmed shortly.

He studied her heart-shaped face. She was quite lovely, he thought, with flawless skin, a short, straight nose, generous mouth, dark silky hair taken up into a neat coil, and almond eyes beneath winged brows the deep, purple-blue of pansies.

Eyes that at the moment were sparkling with anger.

It had been his intention to leave—his company's new lawyer would be taking up her post in ten days' time, and at a pinch his business could wait—but all at once he changed his mind.

This woman interested and intrigued him. As well as beauty, she had brains, character and spirit.

She also had a temper.

Deciding to test that temper a little more, he said, 'I see.' Glancing at her from beneath long, gold-tipped lashes, he added, 'Well, if you think you can cope...?'

Forcing back an angry response, she said, 'I can cope.'

'Then the answer to your question is, no.'

She took a deep, steadying breath, before saying coolly, 'Well, if you intend to stay, Mr Devereux, perhaps you'd like to sit down?'

Ignoring the chair, he came and sat on the edge of the desk, turning slightly to face her.

Suddenly he was much too close and instinctively she flinched away.

It was only the slightest movement, but he noticed it and looked amused.

This time she kept her cool, but her hand itched to throw something at him.

And he knew it, damn him. In fact the gleam in his eye gave her the distinct impression that he was enjoying needling her.

Before she could make any attempt to regain the initiative, he asked with smooth effrontery, 'So after only a year, and young as you are, you've been offered a partnership? You must be exceptionally clever and talented.'

A flush rising in her cheeks, she said tightly, 'I don't claim to be either of those, Mr Devereux. But I graduated from one of the top English law schools with honours, and while I've been with the firm I've kept studying and learning.'

Her voice as dispassionate as she could make it, she went on, 'If you knew my father and my uncle at all well, you would know that they have no time for nepotism. *Any* advancement in this firm has to be earned by hard work and competence.'

Yes, she certainly had a temper, but she knew how to control it, he thought admiringly.

Deciding to change tactics, he slid off the desk and turned to face her in one fluid movement.

When green eyes met deep blue, he said simply, 'I apologize. While I believe I have every right to be angry, I shouldn't have vented it on you.'

She wanted to say, *no you shouldn't.* Instead, the wind taken out of her sails, she said inanely, 'That's all right.'

'Forgive me?'

'Of course.'

He gave her a smile that lit his eyes, put creases beside his mouth and sent his already powerful sex appeal soaring. 'And you're not still angry with me?'

That smile robbed her of breath and, unable to speak, she shook her head.

'Positive?'

'Yes, I'm positive,' she managed.

His gaze dropped to her hands which were long and slim with neat oval nails, mercifully free from the dark-coloured varnishes he so disliked.

Pleased that she appeared to be neither married nor engaged, he asked, 'Are you doing anything tonight?'

Taken by surprise, she echoed, 'Doing anything?'

'I mean do you have a date with a boyfriend, or a live-in lover waiting impatiently at home for you?'

'Neither.'

'Why not? A beautiful woman like you.'

'For the last five years I've been working so hard I've had no time for boyfriends or live-in lovers,' she told him pointedly.

Suddenly human and likeable, he pulled a droll face. 'I suppose I asked for that.'

'You did, rather.'

'Well, now you've cut me down to size, how about having dinner with me tonight?'

Feeling a strange pang of regret, she said, 'I'm afraid I can't. I'm driving down to Catona tonight to start my vacation.'

'Are you meeting someone there?'

'I'm staying with a friend.'

'Oh?' He raised a questioning brow.

For no good reason, she found herself explaining, 'Sam's an old school friend.'

'Male or female?'

'Female.'

'I see.' He looked satisfied. 'What time is she expecting you?'

'No particular time. Whenever I get there.'

'Well Catona's only a couple of hours away at the most. You could always have dinner with me first. After all, you'll need to eat some time,' he pointed out persuasively.

As Caris hesitated, he added, 'If you don't say yes, I'll know you haven't forgiven me.'

'But I *have* forgiven you.'

He smiled into her eyes. 'Then tell me where you live and I'll pick you up at...shall we say seven?'

Without intending to, Caris found herself telling him, 'I live in Apartment One-A, Lampton House, Darlington Square.'

She was about to explain how to find it when he said cheerfully, 'I know Darlington Square. I have a small apartment quite near there.

'Until seven, then.' He sketched a brief salute and was gone.

She must be stark, staring mad! she thought, gazing after him. Pressure of work had meant burning the midnight oil for the past couple of weeks, and she had intended to get to Catona in time to have an early night tonight.

So what on earth had made her agree to go out with a man she had only just met, and whose first name she didn't even know? A man who had proved he could be not only difficult but downright demoralizing? A man she had felt instinctively was dangerous?

The truth was she had found him damn-nigh irresistible, and that element of danger added a dash of excitement and spice that had been sadly missing from her life.

When her doorbell rang promptly at seven, Caris was ready and organized, her evening bag and jacket to hand, her small vacation case and holdall packed and waiting to be put into her car later.

With no idea where he intended to take her, she had been undecided what to wear. In the end, having little else because she so rarely went out, she had put on her one and only cock-tail dress, a silky sheath in midnight blue with matching high-heeled strappy sandals.

Needing little in the way of make-up, she had applied a light foundation and a touch of lip gloss, taken her hair up into an elegant chignon and fastened pearl drops to her small lobes.

As she opened the door she wondered if he would approve. She very much hoped so.

His gaze travelled over her slowly and appreciatively. Now she had shed the formal business suit, he could see that, as well as a lovely face, this woman had a stunning figure.

Seeing the open admiration in his eyes Caris was satisfied that he liked what he saw.

Knowing now how attractive he was, she had thought herself prepared, and hadn't expected to be bowled over by the sight of him. But, looking more handsome than ever in an immaculate dinner jacket and black tie, he made her heart lurch crazily.

Taking a deep breath, she invited, 'If you'd like to come in for a moment, Mr Devereux…?'

'Won't you call me Zander? Everyone else does.'

'Zander?' she echoed uncertainly.

'A mistake on my birth certificate,' he explained with a twinkle in his eye. 'My parents had intended to call me Alexander, but somehow Zander went down and the name stuck.'

Following her into the light, pleasantly furnished living-room, he remarked with a smile, 'A nice place. Do you live here alone?'

'No, I share. But Mitch is on vacation in Rome and won't be back for another week.'

'Mitch?'

'Diana Mitchell, but everyone calls her Mitch.'

Then, recalling the time, Caris added hastily, 'I'm all ready. I just need pick up my jacket and bag.'

'It's a pleasure to find a woman who's prompt as well as beautiful.'

His words sent a little thrill of excitement running through her. But, knowing it was necessary to keep her feet firmly on the ground, she observed practically, 'I need to be prompt. I'm hoping to be back here in time to put my luggage in the car and get down to Catona this side of midnight.'

Glancing at the waiting case and holdall, he asked thoughtfully, 'Will you be doing much driving while you're there?'

She shook her head. 'None at all, I imagine. First thing

tomorrow morning, Sam and I will be joining a small group of hikers who'll be doing a five-day trek along the Rowton Way. But I need my car to get to Catona and back.'

'If that's all, I've a suggestion to make. The restaurant I'm planning to take you to is well on the way to Catona.'

Feeling suddenly breathless, she waited, wondering what was coming.

'So, if we take your luggage with us, after we've eaten instead of bringing you back here I could drive you down to your friend's. That would save a good deal of time.'

'Oh, but...'

'It would give us the chance to be together longer and have a more leisurely meal.'

The chance to be together longer...

Her heart doing strange things, she pointed out, 'But then I wouldn't have a car to get back.'

'My house is only about twelve miles from Catona, so if you let me know when your vacation's over I could quite easily pick you up.'

'I couldn't possibly put you to all that trouble,' she protested.

'It's no trouble. If it had been I wouldn't have suggested it.' Briskly, he added, 'Is this all the luggage you have?'

'Yes.'

'Is there anything else you need to do before we go?'

Common sense told her she ought to dig her toes in and refuse to be hustled but, looking into those green eyes, she was lost.

'Nothing else,' she answered.

He put her jacket around her shoulders and handed her her bag, before picking up her case and holdall. 'Then let's get started.'

Feeling as if she was being swept along by a prairie wind,

Caris allowed herself to be escorted out to a sleek silver sports car that waited by the kerb.

When her luggage had been stowed in the back and she had been helped into the passenger seat, Zander slid behind the wheel. 'All set?'

She nodded.

The engine purred like a satisfied cat; they traversed the quiet square and joined the busy evening stream of traffic.

Some five minutes later they had left the outskirts of the city behind them and were heading roughly south-west.

Seeing the wooded peaks of the Catskills in the distance, she asked, 'Where exactly are we going?'

'The restaurant is called Le Jardin Romarin. It's rather a special place, and they have an excellent French chef.'

'How far is it?'

'Not too far. It's near the mountains, on the outskirts of a pretty little village called Bright Angel Falls.'

'Oh, we once drove through Bright Angel Falls!' she exclaimed. 'I remembered it because it was such a lovely name.'

'Do you know the area well?'

'Not very well. But my father took me that way once or twice when I was younger, and I always thought it was really picturesque.'

'So it is,' he agreed. 'That's why I chose to buy a house in that area.'

If he had a house, as well as an apartment in town and a luxury car, he must be a relatively wealthy man; the way he dressed seemed to confirm that.

But, even if he hadn't had a cent, with his looks and charisma it was a wonder he was still free.

They were following a quiet, spruce-lined road when he broke into her thoughts to remark, 'We'll soon be at the bridge that spans the Bright Angel Gorge. If you look to your left, you'll get a good view of the falls. They're quite spectacular.'

When they dropped down an incline, Caris saw the bridge ahead of them, and on the opposite side a small parking area from which a short but steep and narrow flight of rocky steps led down to a viewpoint guarded by a chest-high railing.

As they crossed the bridge, she glanced left, as she had been bidden. A series of delicate waterfalls, looking like skeins of bright spun silk, plummeted gracefully into the rocky depths; lit by the rays of the sinking sun, a rainbow arched in the air, forming a multicoloured halo.

Her first thought was that he had been right to call them spectacular. In fact even that adjective seemed to be something of an understatement.

When he glanced at her, as if trying to judge her reaction, she said a little huskily, 'They're magnificent. Absolutely magnificent.'

'So is the gorge itself. But it's so deep you can only see it properly by going down to the viewpoint.'

'Could we do that? Have we time?'

'If you want to go down, we'll make time.' As he spoke, he was drawing into the car park.

Having helped her from the car, he warned, 'Better let me go first. Some of the steps are worn and uneven, and could be tricky with those high heels.' Carefully, she followed him down and, standing by the railings, looked over into the gorge.

The tumbled rocks and surging white water far below took her breath away, and she was still gazing in wonder when her companion reminded her, 'If you want to get down to Catona tonight we'd better be moving.'

The awesome scene still filling her mind, she held on to the metal handrail and began to climb back up the steps, Zander at her heels.

She had almost reached the top when she missed her footing and slipped off a step.

Her companion stopped her falling and held her steady

until she'd had time to gather herself, before asking, 'Any damage done?'

'No, I don't think so,' she answered.

But when she tried to climb the remaining steps she couldn't prevent a gasp of pain.

'What is it?'

Reluctantly, she admitted, 'I'm afraid I've twisted my ankle.'

CHAPTER TWO

'HOLD on,' he instructed, and squeezed past her. 'Now then, put your free arm around my neck.'

She obeyed and, lifting her clear of the steps, he swung her up into his arms.

Though he was no stranger to women, he was unprepared for how the weight of her slim yet curvaceous body lying against his set his heart beating faster.

For her part, Caris felt distinctly awkward. Being carried was an unfamiliar sensation for a woman of five feet seven who weighed a hundred and thirty pounds and she was pleased they had the place to themselves so there was no one to stare.

After a moment or two the awkwardness passed. He bore her weight with such ease that by the time they reached the car she was starting to feel safe, protected and *feminine*, and to quite like the novel experience.

When she was settled on the front passenger seat, he crouched to pull off her sandal and examine her left ankle and foot. As his long fingers probed, she couldn't prevent a wince.

He glanced up sharply.

'It's all right,' she assured him.

His examination over, he reported, 'There doesn't seem

to be anything broken, but it's started to swell already, and it's my guess that you have quite a nasty sprain.'

Then, his tone vexed, 'I'm an absolute fool! I should have had more sense than take you down there in those heels.'

'It isn't your fault,' she assured him quickly. 'I should have had more sense than go down. But I wouldn't have missed it for the world. And it's really not too painful.'

As she moved her foot experimentally, a stab of agony made her gasp, giving the lie to her words.

'Take your stocking off,' he instructed. 'I've a first-aid box in the trunk.'

While he was gone, on the grounds that it was better to have bare legs than be odd, she took off both her stockings and put them in her purse.

He returned after a moment or two with the box and, having applied an analgesic spray and a crepe bandage, asked, 'How does it feel now?'

'Much better, thank you,' she replied cheerfully as she slipped her sandals back on and swung her legs into the car.

'That's good. Though I doubt if you'll be doing much serious walking for a few days.'

'Oh Lord!' In the excitement of the moment, she had given scant thought to her vacation.

'I suppose I ought to warn Sam that I may not be able to join the group. But I don't want to disappoint her unless I'm forced to.'

'Then why not wait until we get to the restaurant?' Zander suggested. 'If you leave it for a while you may have a better idea of just how much of a problem the ankle's going to be.'

'You're right, of course.'

When he had slammed the car door, he replaced the first-aid box and got behind the wheel.

As he drove, his thoughts were busy. It was odds on that her ankle would prevent her from joining a trekking party, but would she still want to join her friend in Catona?

He rather hoped not. Past experience told him she was already attracted to him, and he couldn't wait to get her into bed.

With a lot of women it would have been easy—too easy, in fact. Most of them had been so over-eager he'd soon become bored and only too keen to bring things to an end.

But already he felt certain that this woman was different. Rather than being the worldly, extrovert, anything-goes type, she was quiet and self-contained and, beneath what he guessed was normally a cool, composed exterior, maybe even a little shy.

Suddenly he was looking forward to finding out, filled with anticipation at the thought of getting to know her a whole lot better. Of holding her in his arms and making love to her.

Smiling wryly to himself, he realized he hadn't felt this interested and eager since he had been a lanky seventeen-year-old and really enamoured of the pretty girl who lived across the way.

By the time they reached their destination the sun had disappeared behind the wooded peaks, and the air was the clear piercing blue that in mountainous regions reigns briefly between sunset and dusk.

'Here we are,' Zander said as he came round to help her out. 'Le Jardin Romarin.'

It was an old and picturesque building, with a jumble of pitched roofs and sloping gables. On each side of the stone steps leading up to the imposing entrance were tubs of spiky purple lavender and dark, glossy rosemary.

'Careful now,' he warned as she gathered up her purse and jacket and swung her feet to the ground.

Favouring her bad ankle, she stood up cautiously; so far so good. But when she tried to put weight on it she was unable to prevent an exclamation of pain. 'Bad, huh?' he said sympathetically.

'I don't think I can walk,' she admitted.

'Then put your arms round my neck.'

A sudden excitement surging through her, she obeyed, and once again found herself being swung up and held against a broad chest.

This time she felt less awkward about being carried, but was more affected by it.

She could feel the warmth of his body, the solidness of the bone and muscle she rested against, and, mingling with the clean masculine scent of his skin, the tangy aftershave he used.

Their faces were so near to one another that she could see the faint laughter lines at the corners of his eyes, and a small, vertical scar by the side of his mouth.

Such close contact sent a shiver of excitement through her, made breathing difficult, and set her heart beating faster.

The door was opened for them and, having climbed the steps seemingly without effort, he carried her into an elegant foyer-bar where a small party of people were enjoying a drink while they waited for their table.

Embarrassment washed over her, but when no one as much as glanced their way her discomfort faded.

Feeling her relax, Zander asked, 'Satisfied I won't drop you?'

Seeing her cheeks grow pink, and finding it a sweet amusement to tease her, he added wickedly, 'Or are you starting to enjoy being carried?'

She was saved from having to answer by a sturdy, silver-haired man wearing a dinner jacket and black bow-tie who crossed the foyer to greet them.

'Zander, nice to see you again, *mon ami*!' he exclaimed jovially.

'Nice to see you, Claude.'

With an unmistakable twinkle in his eye, the Frenchman asked, 'Do I take it that you and *madame* are enjoying a *lune de miel*?'

'Unfortunately not. I'm afraid mademoiselle has hurt her ankle.'

Claude tutted his concern. 'Then we will have to try and make up for it with one of our best tables and an especially good meal.'

He led the way through French doors to a rear veranda and over to a secluded table, beautifully set with a low centrepiece of apricot-coloured roses and a squat gold candle.

'Now do please make yourselves comfortable.'

As soon as Caris had been settled in a chair, an attentive waiter relieved her of her jacket and whisked it away.

Nodding his approval, Claude went on, 'I will send along a bottle of our best champagne, and if you care to leave the choice of menu in my hands…?'

After giving Caris a questioning glance and receiving her nod of agreement, Zander answered, 'Thanks, Claude, we'll be happy to.'

'Then I will see that chef excels himself on your behalf. Oh, one last thing…' Turning to Caris he asked, 'Would *mademoiselle* like something to rest her injured foot on?'

A little flustered by so much attention, Caris said, 'Thank you, but it's really not necessary.'

With a smile and an inclination of his head, the Frenchman hurried away.

The lantern-hung veranda overlooked a steeply terraced garden with winding steps and secret paths, stone benches and pale statues in arbours. Water cascaded over tumbling rocks into fern-hung pools, and dark, glossy rosemary seemed to grow in every nook and cranny.

A solitary bright evening star and a velvety-blue dusk waiting in the wings made the scene seem magical, enchanted.

It set the atmosphere for the whole evening.

Having gazed her fill, Caris remarked, 'This is a lovely place in a lovely setting.'

'I rather hoped you'd like it,' Zander admitted.

As she moved her foot into a more comfortable position he said, 'Sure you don't need a cushion? Raising it might help to ease the pain and prevent swelling.'

She shook her head. 'It only hurts when I put weight on it, and the swelling seems to have stopped. Though I think you were right about the trekking.'

'Then this might be a good time to call your friend and put her in the picture.'

She sighed. 'Walking the Rowton Way is something Sam's been really looking forward to.'

'So what do you intend to do?'

'Stay in Albany,' Caris said decidedly. 'I don't want her to call it off on my account, which is what she'll do if I'm in Catona and not able to go.'

Fishing out her mobile phone, she tapped in the number. After a moment or two she frowned. 'I'm not getting any answer, which is odd… Oh, wait a minute, I have a text message from her.

'Oh Lord, she has an even worse problem than I do. Her widowed mother's been taken ill and she's having to fly up to Boston to nurse her. She says to go on the trek without her, so I'd better let her know how things are…'

The text sent, Caris dropped the phone back into her bag. 'I'm sorry about that.'

'There's no need to be. It had to be settled. But it's a pity about your vacation.'

Hiding her disappointment, she said lightly, 'Oh well, it can't be helped. I'll just have a quiet time at home.

'If I get bored I can always go into the office or ask Kate to drop some work round. There's always plenty to do.'

At that moment, the wine waiter approached wheeling a trolley. He stooped and with a click of his lighter lit the candle. Then, having stationed the trolley to his satisfaction, he twirled the bottle of Dom Perignon in its ice bucket and began the little ceremony of opening and pouring the vintage champagne.

'Go easy on mine,' Zander said as the wine bubbled into the flutes. 'I'll be driving later.'

When the napkin-wrapped bottle had been replaced in the bucket and the waiter had moved away, Zander lifted his glass in a toast. 'Here's to us, Caris, and getting to know one another better.'

'To us,' she echoed.

Those fascinating green eyes of his fixed on her face. He remarked, 'You have an unusual name. Who chose it?'

'My mother.'

'Caris,' he murmured softly, making the word sound like a caress. 'It suits you.'

As she sipped the champagne, emboldened by his toast and wanting to know more about him, she asked, 'What kind of work do you do?'

'I'm in the hotel business.'

Of course; she had wondered why the name seemed to be familiar. Now she recalled glancing through a society magazine and reading about the aristocratic Devereux family.

'I thought I knew the name. Devereux Hotels are famous all over the globe. I read in one of the glossy magazines that it's been a family concern for more than a hundred years.'

'Yes. It all started with my great-grandfather, Gerald Devereux.'

'Wasn't he the younger brother of a duke?'

'Yes, but he stopped using his title when he married an American and came to live in the States. Originally he set up his own merchant bank in London, then in the late eighteen-hundreds he acquired a hotel as a bad debt. That sparked his interest and as a business proposition he began to build more.'

'So do you run the business?'

'No, my father does.'

'James Devereux?'

'That's right.'

The article had gone on to say that James Devereux, a multimillionaire who owned a chain of five-star hotels worldwide, had been happily married to the same woman for almost forty years.

His son, on the other hand, appeared to be a Casanova, noted for his many high-profile affairs and his ability to remain a bachelor despite the amount of women trying to catch him.

Zander was going on. 'I'm an architect by training and inclination, so I spend a lot of my time designing and building new hotels or converting existing properties.'

'In the States?'

'Worldwide.'

'Which means you do a lot of travelling?'

'A fair amount.'

'Lucky you. Do you have a favourite country?'

'I have a soft spot for England,' he admitted.

'Then you know it well?'

'Very well. I was born in London and I went to Oxford. You see, though my father is American by birth, my mother, who died last year, was English.'

'I'm sorry for your loss,' Caris said. 'That is strange, though, as I have an American father and an English mother.'

'So where were you born?'

'A little market town called Spitewinter, on the Cambridgeshire border. My grandfather was the vicar there. I got my law degree at Cambridge University.'

'What made you decide on law as a career?'

'It was decided for me. It wasn't something I wanted to do. You see, my father had hoped for a son to follow in his footsteps, but it wasn't to be. My mother died when I was quite young.'

'And your father never married again?'

Caris shook her head. 'He'd adored my mother and he never really got over her death. He became morose and bitter.'

'But you must have been a comfort to him.'

'Quite the reverse, apparently. I was left in the care of various nannies and sent away to boarding school as soon as I was old enough to go. But, later on, when I proved to be reasonably bright, it became my father's dearest wish that I should train to be a lawyer and join the firm.'

'Why did you choose to go to Cambridge?'

'Once again, the decision was made for me. Though my father is American born and bred, his family, as well as my mother's, were originally from Cambridgeshire.'

'How did they end up in the States?'

'In the early eighteen-hundreds one of our ancestors emigrated and settled in New Jersey, but he sent his eldest son back to England to finish his education at Cambridge. Since then it's become a kind of family tradition that in each generation the eldest son of the eldest son should go there.

'My father went. That's where he met and fell in love with my mother. She was a law student too, but in her second year she was forced to leave when she became pregnant. They got married as soon as they knew, and I was born at my grandparents' house in Spitewinter.

'Shortly afterwards, my father graduated and took my mother and me back to the States with him. But it hadn't been an easy birth—something had gone wrong—and she never fully recovered. After she died, he could scarcely bear to look at me. It was almost as if he blamed me for her death.'

'I see,' Zander said slowly. 'But, now you've taken the place of the son he never had, presumably you've grown closer?'

Caris shook her head regretfully. 'I'm afraid you could never call the relationship I have with my father *close*.'

'But you get on okay with him as a rule?'

'Reasonably well, while I'm willing to be a dutiful daughter and not cross him.'

Zander frowned. 'I find it difficult to believe he's not proud of you.'

'Perhaps he is, a little. But I've still got a long way to go to get where he wants me to be.'

'Where's that?'

'It's his dream that one day I'll become a top-class barrister.'

'Really?'

'Don't sound so surprised.'

'I wouldn't have figured you as a barrister.'

'You don't think I have the brains?'

'Such a thought never entered my head. It's just that I've always considered a top-class barrister must have a certain hardness, the ability to remain detached, uninvolved emotionally.

'I can easily believe you're level-headed and clever but, though I still don't know you well, I have a gut feeling that you're too tender-hearted to make it a comfortable profession.'

'Now should I be flattered or insulted?' she wondered aloud.

He laughed. 'Please, take it as a compliment.'

At that moment their first course arrived. It proved to be a very tasty lobster bisque, and apart from an occasional remark they fell silent as they did justice to it.

It was followed by a tender steak served with a delicious *cheureuil* sauce, and they ended with a fruit and cream cheesecake that was light as a dream. As soon as their plates had been whisked away, the attentive waiter brought coffee, chocolates and a small trolley holding a selection of liqueurs.

'Which would you prefer?' Zander asked. 'Brandy? Cointreau? Benedictine?'

'I like Benedictine,' Caris admitted. 'But as I've already had at least two glasses of champagne I'm not sure if it would be wise.'

'Well, as you won't be driving, I can't see the harm. And it may help you get a good night's sleep in spite of the ankle.'

Taking that as a yes, the waiter poured a generous amount of Benedictine into one of the glasses. Then with the bottle poised he enquired, 'And for you, sir?'

Zander shook his head. 'Nothing for me, thanks.'

When the waiter had departed, with no need for small talk they sipped their coffee in companionable silence, looking out over the dusky garden.

A warm evening breeze drifted by, carrying with it the fragrance of roses, lavender and the haunting scent of rosemary.

With a sigh, Caris turned to her host and said, 'That was the best meal I can ever remember having.'

In the flickering candlelight, Zander smiled at her. 'I'm glad you enjoyed it.'

He had good teeth—nicely shaped, gleaming white and healthy—and his mouth was beautiful, she thought, the top lip ascetic, the fuller lower lip more sensuous.

She was still staring, caught by the sexiness of it, when he added approvingly, 'It's a pleasure to have dinner with a woman who appreciates good food and doesn't want to chatter all through the meal.'

Floating on cloud nine, happy that he seemed to like her company and hadn't found her silence dull, Caris glowed.

She already knew that she would always remember this lovely, romantic evening. An evening she never wanted to end.

But her father was a hard taskmaster; for the past few

weeks, needing to get things done before her vacation, she had worked far into the night most nights and slept badly in consequence.

Now tiredness was starting to catch up with her, made even more soporific by too much alcohol; she found herself having to stifle a yawn.

Zander noticed at once. 'About ready to go?' he queried. 'It's getting late and you look tired.'

'Yes, I'm ready.' She managed a smile.

But after such a wonderful evening to return to her lonely apartment with its empty fridge and stripped bed seemed like a complete anti-climax, and her heart felt like lead.

'Or perhaps you'd rather not go home tonight? It won't be much fun going back to an empty apartment so late, especially with an injured ankle and no holiday to look forward to…'

Surprised by the way he had picked up so accurately what she was thinking and feeling, she asked, 'How long have you been psychic?'

'So I guessed right? You don't want to go home?'

As lightly as possible, she said, 'I don't have much choice now I'm not going to Catona.'

'Why not spend the night at my house?'

As her head came up, he added, 'I ought to make it clear that this isn't an indecent proposal. But as you don't want to go home—'

Horrified in case he thought she had been angling for an invitation, she broke in sharply. 'Oh no, I couldn't possibly.'

'Why not?'

'I just couldn't.' Uncomfortably, she added, 'I didn't mean to sound as if I was…'

On her wavelength immediately, he heaved a mock sigh. 'That's a pity. I was rather hoping you wanted my company as much as I wanted yours. However, if you don't, there's always the river.'

Smiling in spite of herself, she said, 'I just didn't want you to think I was—'

'I didn't think anything of the kind. But, if by any chance I *had*, I assure you I would have been extremely flattered. So do come.'

'I really couldn't put you to so much trouble,' she protested thickly.

'It's no trouble. Hallgarth has a perfectly good guest room, which my housekeeper always leaves made up, and we can be there in less than half an hour.'

Persuasively, he added, 'Say yes, and after you've enjoyed a good night's sleep we can have breakfast together before I take you home.'

Under normal circumstances, common sense would have insisted that she should say no and mean it. But too much alcohol had swamped both her usual reserve and her inhibitions. If truth be told, she was curious to see his house.

After a brief hesitation, she threw caution to the winds and agreed, 'Very well, I'll come.'

He smiled, a white, attractive smile that creased his lean cheeks and made her heart give a little lurch. 'That's good.'

Watching her stifle yet another yawn, he signalled to the waiter to bring her jacket, adding, 'If I don't get you home soon, you'll be fast asleep.'

When he had paid the bill and added a generous tip, he lifted her into his arms.

At that moment Claude appeared and beamed at them. 'I hope you have enjoyed a good meal and had a pleasant evening?'

'We can answer a resounding yes to both those questions,' Zander told him.

'Then you must both come again as my guests.'

'We'll look forward to it.'

Their thanks and goodbyes said, they made their way out to the car.

When Caris was settled in the front passenger seat, Zander got behind the wheel and fastened both their seatbelts. In a matter of seconds they had left the lighted restaurant behind them.

Only when they were travelling down a deserted, tree-lined road, their headlights groping through the darkness like the luminous antennae of some insect, did she have second thoughts about the wisdom of what she was doing.

After all, it was far from sensible behaviour to go off into the blue with a man she scarcely knew, a man who, though he had talked about a housekeeper and a guest room, had a reputation as a Casanova.

As though he sensed her sudden unease, he glanced side-ways at her in the weird, unearthly light from the dashboard.

'Something wrong?'

'No, not really...' she mumbled.

'I thought you might perhaps be regretting your decision to come?'

Her silence effectively answered his question.

'What are you afraid of? That I might turn out to be a hom-icidal maniac?'

'Of course not!'

'Then you're scared I'll twirl an imaginary moustache and whisk you off into the woods like some pantomime villain?'

'Hardly.'

'But that's closer to the mark?'

Once again her silence spoke for her.

He sighed. 'I frankly admit that if you do want to share my bed I'll be delighted. But, if you don't, then you'll be as safe as if you were in a nunnery.'

Though his tone was quizzical, her every instinct told her that he spoke the exact truth.

More seriously, he went on, 'If I haven't managed to set your mind at rest, and you really *don't* trust me, say so at once and I'll be happy to turn round and take you home.'

'I do trust you. Implicitly,' she added.

'Thank you for that.'

He drove in silence for a while, then as they took the road that climbed steadily into the mountains he slanted her a glance.

She was asleep, her thick lashes making dark fans on her high cheekbones, her lovely mouth slightly parted. She looked both alluring and vulnerable, and he felt a strong urge to stop the car and kiss her.

When they reached Hallgarth and drew up in the pool of light cast by the porch lantern, she was still sound asleep.

Reluctant to disturb her, he left her where she was while he took her case and holdall up to the pleasant but seldom-used guest room.

Returning to the car, he lifted her out carefully and carried her up the hickory staircase. Laying her down on the bed, he removed her sandals before settling her dark head on the pillow and pulling up the lightweight duvet.

He had half-expected her to stir and open her eyes, but she remained soundly asleep until he finished his ministrations and left, closing the door quietly behind him.

When Caris awoke, she opened her eyes to a large, pleasant room with light modern furniture and apricot walls. A room that was totally strange to her.

Two long windows hung with fine muslin curtains looked out over well-tended lawns and colourful flowerbeds to a group of white wooden chalet-type buildings. Through a vine-hung trellis she could just glimpse the blue waters of a swimming pool.

For a moment or so she was at a complete loss, with no idea where she was or how she had got there.

Then it all came rushing back—the magical evening she had spent with Zander and his invitation to spend the night at his house.

So that solved the mystery of where she was; she was in Zander Devereux's guest room. But the combination of tiredness and alcohol had zonked her so completely that she had no recollection of the journey, or of arriving here.

She was still wearing her dress, and her jacket was hung neatly over a nearby chair. Her evening bag was lying on the bedside table.

She must have his housekeeper to thank.

Wondering how long she had slept, she looked at her watch a little blearily and found it was mid-morning.

She still felt slightly muzzy from the unaccustomed drink, but a refreshing shower would help to clear her head and set her to rights.

Galvanized into action, she pushed back the duvet and swung her feet to the floor.

After removing the bandage and cautiously trying out her injured ankle, she found it was less painful than she had expected and she could just about walk on it with care.

The pale grey carpet was soft as smoke beneath her bare feet as she crossed to where her luggage had been placed on a low chest.

When she had found her toilet things and a change of clothing, she made her cautious way to the sumptuous *en suite* bathroom, with its mirrored walls and off-white carpet.

There she found a luxurious bathtub and shower, and on a glass shelf an array of toiletries, towels and a pair of folded bathrobes.

By the time she stepped out of the shower the hot water had done its work; her head had cleared and she was feeling altogether brighter.

Wearing one of the bathrobes, she brushed her teeth and blow-dried her long hair, leaving it loose around her shoulders before returning to the bedroom.

Having donned clean undies, a silky dress that echoed the turquoise, green and gold of a tropical sea, and flat-heeled sandals, she swapped her evening bag for her handbag, which she'd put in her holdall, and repacked her case.

Then, leaving her bag and a lightweight jacket on top of the case, she ventured onto the landing. She was suddenly filled with excitement and anticipation at the thought of seeing Zander again. She made her way down the graceful curve of stairs to a spacious hall, with doors leading off on either side.

Right at the far end, through a partially open door, she could see a small but well-equipped gym but it appeared to be empty.

Everywhere was silent and, with no one about to ask, she went to the nearest door and tapped lightly on it.

She struck lucky the first time. Her knock was answered by Zander's voice calling, 'Come in.'

Wondering if he would have the same powerful impact she recalled from the previous evening, she walked into an office full of state-of-the-art technology.

Looking fresh and strikingly attractive in an olive-green silk shirt, short-sleeved and open at the neck, he was sitting behind a desk working with a laptop. A lock of his thick blond hair, which was parted on the left and cut fairly short, hung over his forehead.

When he glanced up, and those eyes met hers—those fascinating green eyes—she found it difficult to breathe.

Which effectively answered her question.

Rising to his feet, he brushed back the stray lock and, with a smile that stopped her breath completely, said, 'Ah, so you're up. When I checked on you a little while ago, you were still sleeping soundly. How are you feeling this morning?'

Somehow she dragged air into her lungs and managed, 'I'm fine, thank you.' Seeing him start to shut down the computer, she added in a rush, 'Please don't stop work on my account.'

'I've done all I need to do. How's the ankle?'

'Oh, much easier.'

He frowned. 'It still looks a little swollen. I'd better put another bandage on it. But first I presume you could do with a drink of some kind?'

'I certainly could,' she admitted.

'Can you make it through to the kitchen without too much discomfort?'

If she said no, he would carry her; just the thought of being lifted and held in his arms again made her feel almost light-headed.

Pushing aside temptation, she assured him, 'Oh yes, I can manage quite well so long as I'm careful.'

As they crossed the hall he slipped a hand beneath her bare elbow, sending shivers running up and down her spine.

He seemed even taller than she remembered, and somehow his height and the mature width of his shoulders, his sheer masculinity, made her feel dainty and feminine.

The kitchen at Hallgarth was large and airy, with all mod cons, its open windows letting in the sunshine and fresh mountain air.

Comfortable and homely, it was fitted out like a farm-house-style living-kitchen, with hickory furniture and an open range, which at the moment was partially screened by a vase of flame-blue delphiniums and pale-pink scented roses.

Caris had half-expected his housekeeper to be there, but

they seemed to have the place to themselves. Wondering about it, she asked, 'Does your housekeeper live in?'

'Mrs Timmins lives over the garage. But it's her weekend off. I hope you don't mind?'

Flustered to realize *he* must be the one who had put her to bed, she stammered, 'Well, n-no, I… No, of course not.'

He gave her a sidelong glance. 'I realize it would have been much more circumspect if my housekeeper *had* been here, but she's gone up to Buffalo to visit her family.'

Straight-faced, but with a gleam in his eye that suggested he was teasing, he went on, 'If in the circumstances you feel seriously compromised…'

Caris was about to deny any such thing when he finished, 'You can always marry me.'

His words made her heart give a little jump. Managing a laugh, she said with determined lightness, 'That seems a little drastic.'

'You mean you'll settle for less?'

'I'll settle for a cup of coffee.'

He sighed. 'Well, if you change your mind about marrying me, just let me know.'

CHAPTER THREE

HAVING filled a percolator and put it on the electric hob, he took a first-aid box from a cupboard and squatted on the hearthrug at her feet.

'While that heats, suppose I take a look at your ankle?'

Watching her wince as he ran assessing fingers over her ankle and slender foot, he said, 'I think some more spray and another bandage wouldn't go amiss.'

The cold spray was soothing—his nearness anything but— and she quivered inwardly at the thought of those strong, long-fingered hands touching her while she slept.

Her pulse rate going up alarmingly, she did her best to ignore how his stone-coloured trousers pulled tight over his lean hips and muscular thighs. Her stomach clenched and a sweet, languorous heat began to spread through her.

Glancing up at her as she sat to all intents and purposes calm and composed, he felt a sudden desire, a strong urge to pull her into his arms, to kiss her and go on kissing her until he had brought an end to that composure.

In short, he wanted her to be *aware*, as aroused as he was.

Almost from the start he had known that this woman had a powerful, quite unprecedented effect on him. What he didn't know for certain was how she felt about him.

And he badly wanted to.

As he stared at her, he noticed the pulse in her throat was beating visibly, and realized with a surge of triumph that despite her calm appearance *she* was feeling the excitement *he* was feeling too.

It was a heady thought.

With an effort, he leashed his libido. It was too soon, he warned himself. This was neither the time nor the place to make love to her, and anticipation would only increase the pleasure.

The air was still thick with sexual tension, but his impulses were once more firmly under control. His voice was even as he asked, 'Not too tight, I hope?'

Looking down into his lean, tanned face and noticing how his long, thick lashes curled, she assured him huskily, 'No… No, it's perfectly all right, thank you.'

When he had fastened the bandage securely, he replaced her sandal and rose to his feet in one lithe movement. 'Now for some coffee.'

He filled two earthenware mugs and handed her one before taking a seat opposite and stretching out his long legs.

The coffee was hot, strong and fragrant, and Caris sipped it gratefully.

When it was gone, he queried, 'More coffee?'

'Please.'

Having refilled her mug, he said, 'While you drink that, decide what you'd like for brunch.'

Still feeling that sensual heat, and terrified of giving herself away, she tried for the prosaic. 'Who does the cooking when your housekeeper's away?'

'I do.'

Remembering her time at university—when most of her male friends had admitted to living on tinned food, takeaway pizzas and being helpless in the kitchen—she asked, 'Really? Can you cook?'

'Can I *cook*!'

Noting the gleam in his eye, she demanded, 'Well, *can* you?'

'Of course I can.'

'Honestly?'

'Oh ye of little faith.'

'Sorry.'

'I should think so.'

'What kind of thing can you cook?'

'I make a mean omelette.'

'In that case, an omelette would be great.'

With a fresh pot of coffee keeping hot, he quickly set the table before taking a pack of bacon and a bowl of brown eggs from the fridge.

While the bacon grilled, he made a large omelette, golden and puffy. Folding it neatly, he garnished it with rolls of crisp bacon before dividing it between two warm plates.

They ate their meal in a companionable silence, and when her plate was empty Caris thanked him, adding, 'I really enjoyed that.'

'Good. Ready for more coffee?'

Reluctant to tear herself away but afraid of outstaying her welcome, she shook her head. 'I really ought to be going.'

'Why? What's the hurry?'

Trying to put conviction into her voice, she told him, 'I'd really like to get home.'

A glint in his eye, he asked, 'Now, why don't I believe that?'

Vexed that he'd seen through her pretence, she asked tartly, 'Why don't you?'

'You have a very expressive face.'

A little disturbed by that remark—wondering what else she might have inadvertently given away—she felt the colour rise in her cheeks.

With a slight grimace, he said, 'Now I've embarrassed you.'

'Not really,' she denied, sticking to her guns. 'But I really ought to be going.'

'If you're determined, I'll get the car out and drive you back.'

'You're sure I won't be interrupting your work?'

'I've done all I need to do for the moment. I'm now planning to enjoy myself.'

That made her smile. 'I can't believe chauffeuring a strange woman around counts as enjoyment.'

'Surely that depends on the woman?'

She could think of nothing to say to that.

When she stayed mute, he pointed out teasingly, 'That was meant to be a compliment.'

As lightly as possible she said, 'In that case, what can I say but, thank you.'

He pretended to consider. 'You could possibly add, "you're very gallant".'

'I'll be happy to, especially if you were to offer to bring my things downstairs.'

With a grin, he saluted her spirited answer.

Then, his face growing serious, he asked, 'If you go back to Albany, what will you do with yourself?'

'Well, I...'

'Do you really want to hurry home just to sit in an empty flat all weekend?'

Caught on the raw—because that was precisely what she almost certainly would be doing—she said a shade crossly, 'Well, what would you suggest I do?'

'You could always stay here.'

Hurriedly she said, 'Thank you, but I really couldn't.'

'Still not sure you can trust me?'

'It's nothing like that,' she denied.

'Then why can't you stay?'

'I couldn't put on you.'

'A quaint phrase, that, and if it means what I imagine it means—i.e. to impose—then my answer is if I'd thought you were *putting on me* I wouldn't have offered.'

'You might have felt obliged to.'

'Well, I didn't,' he replied shortly. 'And when you get to know me better you'll realize that I don't do anything I don't want to do.'

He smiled at her suddenly, lightening the tension. 'Now, if that's set your mind at rest and you have no other serious objections, please stay. I could use the company.'

She could no longer doubt that he wasn't just being polite, that he really did want her to stay. But she was already in danger of falling under his spell, and it would be tantamount to playing with fire.

And there was another important consideration. A man with all his assets must have scores of women only too eager to make themselves available, and it would crucify her pride to have him think she was one of them.

'Well?' he asked, growing impatient.

Knowing perfectly well that she should say no and run, she found herself saying, 'If you're quite sure, then thank you very much, I'd like to stay. And I *would* like another coffee, please.'

Zander breathed an inward sigh of relief.

As he reached for the coffee pot, a dazzling shaft of sunshine slanted in and fell across his face like a spotlight, making his green eyes gleam like a cat's and turning his brows and lashes to burnished gold.

As she stared at him, mesmerized, he glanced up and caught her eye. Watching the betraying colour rise in her cheeks, he challenged softly, 'Tell me what you're thinking.'

Tearing her gaze away, she lied breathlessly, 'I was just thinking what a beautiful day it is.'

'I agree, it couldn't be better. So when we've had our coffee I suggest we make the most of it.'

As he began to pour, she asked, 'What do you usually do at weekends?'

'If I'm here rather than on my travels I like to be active, so if the weather's good I walk, swim, or play tennis. If it's bad, I work out in the gym, read, or watch a little television. And I mean a *little*,' he added. 'I don't care overmuch for television.'

'Neither do I,' she told him with truth. 'But I've always been a bookworm.'

'Do you swim or play tennis?'

'I do both whenever I can, and I enjoy walking.'

'A woman after my own heart. However, considering the state of your ankle, a drive might be a more sensible option.'

'I'm afraid you're right.'

'What about boats; being on the water—enjoy that?'

'It's not something I've had the chance to try.'

'Then you've never been sailing?'

She shook her head.

'Pity. It can be great fun.'

'I can believe that.'

'When the wind's right I quite often go sailing on Square Lake, which is the highest body of water in this area.'

'Square Lake?' she repeated.

'That's right. I can't imagine how it got its name, because it's anything but square. It has lots of pretty little bays and inlets and it's ringed by mountains.'

'How far away is it?'

'About an hour and a half's drive.'

'Is there a sailing club there?'

'No, but I have my own sailing boat, as well as a motor boat.'

'That must be wonderful.'

Hearing the genuine enthusiasm in her voice, he looked a little surprised. 'You approve of so many outdoor pursuits?'

'Certainly.'

'Most of the women I've known, while they may pay lip-service to the idea, can barely repress a shudder. But then I guessed from the start that you were different.'

Not knowing quite what to say to that, she stayed silent while they finished their coffee.

When their mugs were empty, he asked, 'Now, where would you like to go? Anywhere in particular?'

'I don't mind at all,' she told him. 'Wherever you'd like to take me.'

'Then I propose we have a leisurely run though the mountains in the direction of Square Lake. It's a nice scenic drive, and if we don't get sidetracked you can take a look at *The Loon*.'

'Your sailing boat?'

'That's right. Interested?'

'I certainly am.'

'Good.' Smiling at her, he added, 'Oh, in case it cools off later, which it often does in the mountains, it might be a good idea to take a coat of some kind.'

'I'll go up and fetch one.'

Zander shook his head. 'Tell me exactly what you want and I'll get it when I get mine.'

'The jacket I left on top of my case will do fine… Oh, and the handbag that's with it…'

He returned in a short time with their jackets and her bag. 'About ready?'

She nodded.

He cupped her bare elbow. 'Then we'll get off.'

Her heart still beating fast from the touch of his hand, Caris sat down in one of the comfortable wicker chairs in the shady front porch while Zander went to fetch the car.

His house was a beautiful, white clapboard building with gables, steeply pitched roofs and Virginia creeper climbing its walls and rioting over the veranda rails.

To the left of the parking area was a garage block with spacious living quarters above it, and beyond the garages sloping green lawns ended in a colourful shrubbery and a handsome stand of mature trees.

On the right, a short, flower-bordered drive ran down to a white picket fence with a five-barred gate which gave onto a secluded country road.

Though extremely attractive, the whole set-up was simple and unpretentious. Her host, while undoubtedly wealthy, appeared to be a man who was satisfied with a fairly modest lifestyle.

She was inclined to adjust that judgement somewhat when he reappeared and she saw he had swapped the sports car he had been driving the previous evening for a sleek, open-topped vehicle, the colour of pearly early-morning mist.

Smiling a little at her own naivety, she rose to her feet as it purred to a halt by the veranda steps and Zander jumped out to offer her a hand.

Less than a minute later they were through the open gates and heading west, leaving the scattering of widely spaced neighbouring houses behind them.

She took pleasure in the fresh, sparkling air, the warmth of the sun on their faces and a balmy breeze carrying the scent of wild honeysuckle and myrtle. They climbed higher and deeper into the mountains.

As they purred effortlessly along, he pointed out things he thought might interest her, but for most of the time they just drove in silence.

The route they took was a lovely, scenic one and Caris sat back and enjoyed Zander's company and the beautiful views.

Glancing at his handsome profile, she saw he appeared

relaxed and contented, a slight smile hanging on his lips, his blond, wind-ruffled hair giving him a boyish look.

As though aware of her scrutiny, he turned his head to really smile at her. 'All right?'

'Yes, thank you.' She couldn't remember ever feeling happier, she thought as she smiled back.

For some time they had been climbing steadily, following a high ridge with spectacular views to the valley below. Now they were heading into a forested area, the sun-dappled road winding between rocky outcrops topped by pine and spruce.

'In a few minutes we'll get to the small town of Woodville,' Zander told her. 'Over the past few years it's become something of a Mecca for tourists.'

Woodville turned out to be a pretty little place with shopping facilities for the locals, a range of gift shops for the visitors, and countless tea-rooms spilling their tables onto the sidewalks.

When they reached the centre he pulled into a parking space that had just become vacant, asking, 'Think you can manage a short stroll?'

'Yes, of course.'

'Then we'll have a cup of tea, or if you prefer some fresh fruit.'

He came round to help her out; watching her put her weight on her injured ankle, he queried, 'How does it feel?'

'Almost as good as new,' she told him cheerfully.

'Well take care; the last thing we want is any more damage to it.'

With Caris perforce stepping cautiously, they made their way along the main street until they reached Rip van Winkle's, and there they stopped and sat at a table shaded by a red umbrella.

'How far are we from Square Lake?' she asked her companion as she ate a peach and sucked the sticky juice from her thumb and forefinger.

Watching her, thinking how innocently sexy she looked, he answered abstractedly, 'It's just a few miles further on.'

She was wondering why Zander had chosen to stop for tea at Woodville, as they were so close to their destination, when he added, 'But it's off the beaten track, and not at all commercialized, so it doesn't get many visitors. Apart from a general-store-cum-chandler, which boasts a couple of gasoline pumps and caters for the needs of the people who live on the lake, there are no shops or cafés.'

'Do many people live there?'

'There are log cabins scattered all around the shores, but more than half of them are only occupied in the summer months.'

'It sounds wonderfully quiet and remote.'

'That was what first attracted me to the place, and when one of the log cabins came up for sale I decided to buy it.

'I make sure there's always some food in the freezer so that if I want to spend a weekend there, or I feel like enjoying a few days of solitude, I can just take off. It makes a refreshing change to airports and hotels and all the pressures of modern living.

'When I'm at the cabin, I can sit on the front porch and watch the moon rise over the mountains and the moonbeams play across the surface of the lake. I can walk in the woods in the scented twilight, or get up early to see a dew-drenched sunrise and trails of diaphanous mist lying on the water...'

While Caris listened, entranced, Zander talked about the lake and its environs until, the bill paid, they made their way back to the car.

Once they were out of town and heading away from the well-trodden tourist path, the terrain became wilder, lonelier and even more beautiful.

Eventually they turned off the quiet road and followed a rough track that wound into the woods. On either side vegetation brushed against the car and the trees, a mixture of conifer and deciduous, seemed to press closer and become even more dense, shutting out the sunlight.

Slanting her a glance, Zander remarked, 'This area is still known as Bear Woods, though its namesakes are long gone. It's where the going gets a bit more difficult. I use a four-by-four in winter, but I've driven this car along here often enough, so you don't need to be worried.'

'I wasn't,' she assured him serenely, and earned herself an approving look. Her voice dry, she added, 'Though I'm beginning to understand why not too many visitors come here.'

He laughed. 'Yes, you're quite right. It's this relatively short stretch that helps to keep the crowds away.'

The trees had started to thin, and through them she caught a glimpse of sparkling blue water.

'Almost there,' he said.

Round the next bend the track ended abruptly, leaving them in an open sweep of bay where he brought the car to a halt to give Caris a chance to look at the lovely scene.

It took her breath away.

Over to their left, a clear, shallow creek with a stony bottom emptied itself into the sunlit waters of the lake which was surrounded by trees, its curving bays interspersed with rocky promontories.

Around the shoreline she could just make out an attractive scattering of log cabins, wooden landing stages and moored boats, while the encircling mountains made a stunning backdrop.

There was no wind, and the surface of the lake was so mirror-calm that the reflections in the water weren't disturbed by so much as a ripple.

'Like it?' Zander asked.

She nodded mutely, but her shining eyes said it all; he was well satisfied.

He restarted the car and swung left to ford the creek. After a hundred yards or so through a screen of trees she spotted a log cabin by the lake-shore. It was square and squat, with a single chimney and a railed veranda festooned with climbing roses.

As they drew closer, she could see that steps led up to a covered front porch with a chain-hung swing seat, from where there must be glorious views over the lake.

It was an idyllic spot.

'This is Owl Lodge,' Zander told her as they stopped by the porch steps and he helped her out of the car. 'And there at the end of the jetty are my boats, *The Loon* and *The Swift*.'

Two sleek white boats with graceful black lines skimming down their sides were moored at a long wooden pier that ran out into the lake. One was an elegant sailing boat, its white sails furled, the other a small motor boat.

'I'm afraid there's not enough wind to go sailing,' he went on. 'But if you'd care to go for a trip on the lake we can take *The Swift*.'

'I'd love to!' she said, her voice made husky by pleasure and excitement.

'Great. But first, if you like, I'll show you what little there is of Owl Lodge.'

'Please.'

'Okay with the steps?'

'Oh yes, so long as I go carefully.'

Opening the porch door, he showed her into an attractive, open-plan living area. Brightly woven rugs lay on the polished floorboards and matching folkweave curtains hung at the windows.

To the left, two curving shallow steps led to a kind of dais with built-in storage space and a comfortable-looking double bed.

On the far wall there was a wood-burning stove with a huge stack of logs on either side, and grouped in front of the hearth a couch in soft, natural leather, two cushioned armchairs and a low table.

Caris noticed that a fire had been laid ready in the stove, and there were a couple of oil lamps strategically placed.

On the right were two doors. Throwing open the nearest one, Zander showed her a small but luxurious bathroom which had an electric water-heater and a walk-in shower.

'And through here is the kitchen. As you can see, it boasts a table and chairs, but I usually eat either al fresco or in front of the living-room stove, depending on the weather.'

At first sight the kitchen appeared to be completely rustic. It had a deep porcelain sink with a wooden draining board, and above an old black stove, once again laid ready for lighting, was an old-fashioned clothes airer on a pulley.

Then, in complete contrast, arranged on the opposite wall was an electric cooker, a large fridge-freezer, a microwave, and a washer-dryer.

As she gazed at them, speechless, Zander's white teeth flashed in a grin. 'Though I didn't want to spoil the place, I decided a few mod cons were definitely called for.'

'But how do you run them?'

'There's a small generator housed in one of the storerooms. Ben Burgess, who lives about half a mile up the lake and is here all year round, takes care of it for me.

'At the moment things are a bit dicey. One of the parts needs replacing, so he's having to nurse it along until the new one arrives.'

As they returned to the living room, he asked, 'Would you care for a coffee or anything before we go?'

'I don't think so, thank you.'

'Then, if you're agreeable, when we get back we'll have a drink and something to eat before we start the journey home.'

'That suits me fine.'

Leaving her bag on one of the chairs, she picked up her jacket and followed him out.

He took her arm as they negotiated the steps and crossed the shingle to the landing stage. Very conscious of his touch, she walked the length of the jetty like someone in a dream, feeling the warmth of the sun on her back and glimpsing the clear sparkling water and pebbly bottom through the gaps in the wooden boards.

After he had shown her *The Loon*, Zander jumped lightly into the motor boat and turned to offer her a steadying hand.

When she had been helped in and settled in the stern he cast off, started the motor and, with a low, throaty roar, they were on their way.

The next couple of hours whilst they leisurely explored the lake—which had several small islands and numerous inlets—were amongst the most delightful she had ever spent.

She loved being on the water, loved the sights, sounds and smells—the black-headed loons, the movement of the boat, the scent of pine and the slap of the little wavelets—the whole new experience.

Zander proved to be the perfect companion, interesting, knowledgeable and fun to be with. Yet he knew the value of silence, of leaving time for just looking, time for thought and contemplation.

Caris said very little but, watching her expressive face and those shining pansy-blue eyes, Zander was well aware of what she was thinking and feeling, and her sheer enjoyment helped to increase his own.

By the time they headed back to the landing stage the sun was starting to sink behind a gathering mass of purple cloud, and a sudden breeze was making the tops of the reeds at the water's edge dance.

While she listened to the loons making their strange, wild cries, Caris slipped on her jacket; she was starting to get a little cool.

She noticed that Zander, who was no doubt used to the evening drop in temperature, seemed quite happy with bare arms.

As she glanced at him, he remarked, 'We're somewhat later than I'd expected, and if I'm any judge there'll be a storm before too long. That being the case, when we get back I'll close the roof of the car, then I suggest that instead of stopping to eat we have a quick drink and start on our way.'

Caris sighed. Of course Zander was right. All the same, she couldn't help feeling a bit disappointed that they would be leaving quite so soon.

Letting her imagination run riot, she thought how lovely it would be to sit on the porch swing with Zander in the gathering dusk, his arm around her, her head on his shoulder, listening to the night sounds and watching the moon rise over the lake and the storm clouds gather on the horizon.

But the voice of common sense warned her that merely being here with him was foolish enough, without wishing herself into romantic and highly dangerous situations.

Still, her recalcitrant thoughts pictured them going indoors hand in hand to sit snugly in front of the stove and stare into the leaping flames before he carried her to bed…

Shivering a little, she imagined how it would be—the warmth and intimacy of his touch as his hands moved over her; the sweetness of his kisses, then the passionate bliss of his love-making before they slept in each other's arms.

She imagined how they would wake at sunrise to watch the feathery reeds sparkling with dew and the delicate veils of white mist trailing over the water. How, swearing she was cold, he would take her back to bed to warm her...

The boat bumping lightly against the landing stage brought her back to the present with a start.

Tying up deftly, Zander stepped out and turned to offer Caris his hand. 'Careful, now...'

But his caution came too late. Flustered by her own erotic imaginings, she jumped to her feet too quickly, lost her balance when the boat rocked and went over the side.

She surfaced, coughing and choking, and was floundering, trying to find a footing in waist-deep water when Zander jumped in beside her.

His hands beneath her arms, he steadied her until she found her feet on the pebbly bottom.

'Thank you!' she spluttered.

Brushing aside her thanks, he asked tersely, 'Are you all right?'

Clearing her throat, she assured him, 'Somewhat wet, but apart from that I'm fine.'

'I should have had more sense than take you out in a boat until your ankle was fully mended.'

Pushing back the long, dark hair that hung in dripping rats' tails, she told him, 'It had nothing to do with my ankle. I got up too quickly and lost my balance when the boat rocked. My ankle's fine.'

Her last words were negated by an exclamation of, 'Ouch!' when she tried to take a step and her ankle turned painfully.

Without another word, Zander stooped and lifted her high in his arms. Holding her against his chest, clear of the water, he waded to the shore.

Her clothes had become an icy-cold shroud; starting to shiver, she clenched her teeth to stop them chattering.

Having carried her to the cabin and up the steps, he unfastened the door and shouldered it open. As he headed for the bathroom, leaving a wet trail in their wake, he remarked, 'I think a hot shower is the order of the day. Because of its altitude, the lake's always a lot colder than one might imagine.'

'Yes, I noticed,' she told him in such a heartfelt voice that he was forced to laugh.

Lowering her carefully onto the cork-topped stool, he slipped off her sandals and removed the wet bandage before asking, 'Need any help with the rest?'

'No, no, I can manage,' she assured him hastily.

'Then when I've pulled down the blind I'll leave you to it.'

At the door he paused to say, 'If you look in the cupboard there, you'll find a good supply of towels and a couple of robes.'

Stripping off her saturated clothes, Caris dropped them into the sink then, turning on the shower, she stepped in carefully. When the hot water cascaded over her, dispelling the chill, she gave a little sigh of relief.

But by the time she had borrowed shampoo and washed her hair she was starting to feel guilty. Zander too would be cold and wet and would need a shower, and it was all her fault. If she'd kept her mind on what she was doing instead of indulging in erotic fantasies...

Having towelled herself and dried her hair as quickly as she could, she reached for one of the fleecy robes and pulled it on. It came down almost to her ankles and the shoulders were much too wide, but it felt snug and warm, and when she had rolled up the sleeves it became quite wearable.

She wrung out her clothes as best she could, but still they dripped, so she left them in the sink and limped back to the living room.

The fire was blazing merrily and a pot of coffee was bubbling away on top of the stove, the fragrant aroma filling the air.

Zander was putting milk and coffee mugs on the table, his

shirt plastered to him, his trouser-legs clinging to his thighs and calves.

Flustered by the situation she found herself in, and only too aware of her nakedness beneath the robe, Caris hovered uncertainly.

When he glanced up, she said jerkily, 'I'm done. The bathroom's all yours.'

'Feeling better?'

'Much better, thank you.'

'How's the ankle?'

'Fine, so long as I'm careful. I'm sorry,' she added apologetically. 'But I wasn't sure what to do about my wet clothes.'

'I'll deal with them as soon as I've had a shower,' he promised. 'In the meantime, why don't you come and sit by the fire and have some coffee?'

As soon as she was settled in one of the cushioned armchairs, a mug of coffee in her hand, Zander disappeared into the bathroom.

CHAPTER FOUR

THE cooking grill on top of the stove had been opened to let out more heat, and the room was getting comfortably warm. She noticed that their sodden footwear had been stuffed with paper and propped up against the fender to dry.

It was becoming clear that Zander was both efficient and practical.

The daylight had died and was giving way to dusk as she drank her coffee, sitting, staring into the leaping flames while her thoughts went back over the day she had just spent with him.

It had been a wonderfully happy day, a day she would always remember. Though nothing really momentous or earth-shaking had happened, somehow she felt as if it had.

There had been a bubbling excitement, an awareness of him, that had brought her to life and made all her senses jewel-bright. And right from the word go there had been that strong physical attraction, an attraction she had found difficult to hide.

Perhaps it was simply that her body had grown tired of celibacy and she was responding to a handsome and virile male like any healthy young female?

When she had lived at home, her father had scared away any would-be boyfriends. During her later years at university she had steered clear of the opposite sex, giving as a reason her need to work hard and study.

But it had been more than that.

At eighteen, free for the first time from her father's restrictions, and desperately naive, she had fallen madly in love with a fellow student.

Karl, who had been in his final year, was a charming, blond-haired Lothario from a wealthy and aristocratic family.

All the female students had flocked round him, desperate to attract his attention, while Caris had stayed quietly in the background and worshipped him from afar.

She had been stunned, bowled over, when he had singled her out. And when he'd started dating her she had thought herself the luckiest girl alive.

But once he had seduced her his interest had quickly waned, and he had moved on to the next conquest, leaving her heartbroken.

Only in retrospect did she realize that her heart was still intact and untouched. It was her pride and self-respect that had been flayed.

Still the whole thing had left her sadder and wiser, and not a little bitter about what she saw as her own stupidity.

Ignoring her body's needs, she had thrown up a defensive wall and retired safely behind it.

Until now...

But Zander was also a charming Lothario from a wealthy and aristocratic family, so unless she wanted to repeat her earlier mistake she *must* stay behind that defensive wall...

The bathroom latch clicked and Zander reappeared, startling Caris out of her reverie. His hair was still damp from the shower and he wore an identical robe to hers, though his fitted a good deal better.

Carrying a pile of wet garments, he vanished towards the kitchen, saying over his shoulder, 'I'll see how soon I can get these ready to wear.'

Through the partly open door she heard a click and a faint, continuous hum as the dryer got under way.

A moment later he reappeared and, having turned on the lights and drawn the curtains, remarked, 'I'm afraid it's going to be a somewhat lengthy process; you must be getting hungry?'

'I'm beginning to,' she admitted.

'Then I suggest we change our plans and have supper before we start back. In the meantime would you like another coffee?'

When she refused, he poured himself one, dropped into the chair opposite, leaned back, bare feet crossed negligently at the ankles, and stretched towards the blaze.

As he moved his position, his robe fell away a little, giving a glimpse of firm lower thighs. Though he was perfectly decent, Caris was very aware of his nakedness and felt a sensual heat start to run through her; she looked hastily away.

Studiously keeping her eyes down, she saw that his calves were strong, straight and muscular, with a fine scattering of golden hair; his feet were well-shaped with neatly trimmed nails.

She found herself staring at them. Never before had she thought of feet as being anything other than useful, but his were pleasing to look at, fascinating, even.

Tearing her gaze away only with an effort, she glanced up, straight into green eyes that held a gleam of amusement.

He put his empty coffee mug on the table. His face straight, he remarked, 'Fascinating things, feet, wouldn't you say?'

Feeling a complete fool because he'd picked up her own word as if he'd been reading her thoughts, she lied, 'I was just staring into space rather than looking at anything in particular.'

Then, only too aware that she was blushing furiously and desperate to change the subject, she harked back. 'I still haven't thanked you properly for jumping in to help me.'

He grinned. 'I was about to say any time, but perhaps that wouldn't be tactful.'

Deciding to plough on, she apologized, 'I'm really sorry to have caused you so much trouble.'

'It was no trouble. Accidents will happen.' Half-seriously, he went on, 'I just hope it hasn't put you off boats for life.'

'Certainly not. But it has taught me a valuable lesson: the next time I go in a boat I shall be a great deal more careful.'

Saluting her spirited answer, he remarked, 'Well, that's no bad thing. Now, about ready to eat?'

'I'm ready when you are.'

'Good.' He rose to his feet. 'There's a selection of meals that won't take long to heat in the microwave, so if you want to come and take a look I shall aim to be the perfect host and let you choose.'

She was about to get up and follow him when, without any warning, the lights went out, leaving them in darkness save for the flickering firelight.

'Oh hell!' Zander exclaimed. 'It looks as if the generator has gone, which means that until I can get it fixed the dryer is useless. And it's too late to disturb Ben. He and his wife go to bed quite early.'

Reaching for the matches, he proceeded to light the oil lamps, adding, 'But don't worry. I'll put a match to the kitchen stove and finish drying the clothes on the airer.'

'I'd better see to mine...'

As she started to rise, he pressed her gently back into her chair. A gleam of devilment was in his eye as told her, 'It's okay, I can cope. I'm no stranger to female underwear.'

That she could well believe!

His face a picture of innocence, he added, 'You see, I have a younger sister.'

Ruefully aware that he'd been deliberately teasing her, Caris made no comment as he picked up one of the oil lamps and disappeared.

He returned quite quickly to say, 'Well, the fire's going and the clothes are hung up, but they're bound to take quite a time to dry. In my case that's not such a problem; I have other clothes and shoes here.'

The recollection of her previous discomfort made her give away more than she realized. She demanded crossly, 'If you had other clothes here why didn't you change into them straight away?'

Contriving to look slightly hurt, he answered, 'Well, as I couldn't see anything of mine being of much use to you, I decided you might prefer it if I kept you company.'

Wrong-footed, she bit her lip. It had been thoughtful of him to consider her feelings and appreciate that if he had been fully dressed she might have felt uncomfortable.

As it was, however, she had been even more uncomfortable. But honesty made her admit that it was hardly his fault if she couldn't keep her libido under control.

'Thank you,' she said in a slightly stifled voice. 'That was kind of you.'

Acknowledging her tacit apology, he stooped to check the state of her sandals.

Seeing her look hopeful, he shook his head. 'I very much doubt if either they or your clothes will be wearable before the morning.'

Resuming his seat, he continued thoughtfully, 'That being so, it might make sense to stay the night here. What do you think?'

A rush of mingled apprehension and excitement effectively tied her tongue.

When she failed to answer, he said quickly, 'Don't worry; if you don't care for the idea we'll forget it and manage somehow.'

Finding her voice, she said, 'No, no, it's not that I *mind* staying...' Then with a kind of desperation she went on, 'But there's only one bed.'

'I'll be quite happy to stretch out on the couch.'

When still she hesitated, he pointed out practically, 'Apart from the fact that you won't have the privacy of your own room, it's no different to being at Hallgarth.'

Of course he was quite right. At Hallgarth they had been alone together under the same roof. The only thing that made this different was her earlier erotic imaginings.

But thankfully he knew nothing of those.

Taking a deep breath, she said steadily, 'If you really don't mind sleeping on the couch, I've no objection to staying here.'

He studied her intently. 'Great.'

'In fact, it has to be the most sensible option,' she added for good measure.

Nodding as if well satisfied, he said, 'Well, if you're happy with that?'

'Quite happy…'

'Good morning. Sorry I'm so late.'

The click of the latch and Julie's greeting brought Caris back to the present with a start and she looked up dazedly.

Spawned by her dream, the memories of Zander and their first weekend together had been so real, so vivid that sitting at her desk she had been absorbed in the past to the exclusion of all else.

'Sorry I'm late,' Julie repeated as she put her mac and umbrella in the cloakroom. 'To start with I overslept, and because I still had to pack I didn't have time for breakfast.

'Then, to add insult to injury, the bus I usually catch didn't turn up and I had to stand in the rain for half an hour while I waited for the next one.'

Gathering herself, Caris sympathized. 'It sounds like one of those days.'

'You can say that again,' Julie agreed in a heartfelt voice. 'I told you I was going away for the weekend with Marcus?

Well, he'd agreed to collect my case from home and then pick
me up here tonight after work…'

'So what's the problem?' Caris asked when Julie paused
for breath.

'I'd bought a really nice new case, and this morning when
I looked for it to pack I discovered that Ella had borrowed it
without even asking me.'

Caris sighed inwardly. Julie and her sixteen-year-old sister were frequently in contention.

'So I had to make do with my old one.'

'Why don't you make yourself a slice of toast and some
tea before you start work?' Caris suggested soothingly.

'Just what I need to help me feel human again. Want a
cup?'

'Please.'

'I'll only be a mo…' Julie disappeared into the small staff-
room-cum-kitchen at the back.

After two or three minutes she put her head round the door
and, her mouth full of toast, asked, 'Want to drink it at your
desk?'

Feeling it was unprofessional, it wasn't normally something either of them did. But it was quiet, and with the rain
coming down in buckets likely to remain so.

'Why not?' Caris answered.

Julie reappeared quite quickly with two cups of tea and,
having passed one over, went to sit behind her own desk.

'Something bothering you?' she asked suddenly.

'Bothering me?' Caris echoed. 'No, nothing's bothering
me. Why do you ask?'

'You look…I don't know…sort of dazed, as if you're not
quite with it. When I first walked in you appeared to be miles
away.'

'I was,' Caris admitted. Then with a sudden and quite
unaccustomed desire to confide in somebody she explained,

'Early this morning I had a dream that upset me. Made me think of the past.'

'Want to talk about it?'

One part of her didn't. It was over and done with; best forgotten.

But another part of her needed to face it, to talk about it one last time before she could hopefully lock it away for ever.

As if the whole thing had happened to someone else and she was simply a bystander, emotionally uninvolved, Caris began to tell Julie about her dream, then about her first meeting with Zander. She was fine until she got to the part about the log cabin. At that point her spurious calm totally deserted her and, knowing she couldn't talk about what had happened at Owl Lodge, she stopped speaking abruptly.

Seeing Julie frown, and realizing that the girl suspected rape at the very least, she managed shakily, 'It was absolutely magical, and I fell in love with the place.'

Once again swamped by memories, she stayed silent for so long that Julie probed, 'Am I right in thinking that the place wasn't the only thing you fell in love with?'

Caris nodded.

'Any idea how *he* felt?'

'I'd started to hope and believe he felt the same way about me. He was so *right*, so special, a wonderful, romantic lover—passionate and caring, fun to be with, exactly what I wanted and needed. It was as if I'd waited all my life for him…'

'So what happened? Did he turn out to be married? Some men can be heartless,' Julie added, with all the experience of an eighteen-year-old.

'No, he wasn't married.' Suddenly unable to go on, Caris said huskily, 'It just didn't work out.'

At that precise moment the door opened and a man walked in, making speaker and listener alike jump guiltily.

Stirred into action, Julie whipped away the cups and vanished into the back room, while Caris struggled to pull herself together.

What on earth had she been thinking of, sitting pouring out her heart to Julie like some love-sick teenager when she should have been working?

After looking at a display of properties for sale, the newcomer approached her desk.

With a pleasant smile, Caris listened to his requirements and agreed to show him over two likely houses at his convenience.

By lunchtime she had talked to several more potential buyers, provided whatever information and photographs they requested and arranged at least half a dozen appointments for the following week.

All she needed to do now was decide on the best way to handle that afternoon's viewing.

Normally she said very little, careful to apply no pressure and to allow the various properties to speak for themselves. But the sheer importance of the Gracedieu sale made her wonder if that was the right thing to do; would it be better to adopt a bolder, more positive approach?

She sighed. It would almost certainly depend on what kind of man her new client was. And that she didn't know.

In the past it had always helped her to find out as much as she could about potential purchasers, especially the more important ones.

But Julie had taken this particular phone call while Caris had been out, and the only information the girl had been able to supply was that the new client was a Michael Grayson, and it had been his PA who had rung to make the appointment.

A few cautious enquiries on Caris's part had merely established the fact that Michael Grayson was the big boss of Grayson Holdings. Which didn't give her much to go on.

After eating a takeaway sandwich and drinking a cup of coffee, she freshened up in the small cloakroom.

A glance at her watch told her it was a quarter to one. Her appointment wasn't until two-thirty, but even for the more routine viewings she liked to be early. It gave her a chance to relax and go over all the relevant facts and figures so she had them clear in her mind before her client arrived.

Having checked her appearance, she put all the necessary paperwork into her briefcase, collected her mac and shoulder bag, and braced herself for the task that lay ahead.

Looking up from her computer, Julie said, 'The best of luck. I hope you get a quick sale, though I won't hold my breath. People think twice before spending that kind of money.'

Then more positively she went on, 'Mind you, it only takes one.'

'I'll hold on to that thought,' Caris promised a shade drily as she headed for the door.

Her hand on the latch, she added, 'I'm hoping to be back before your boyfriend calls for you, but if by any chance I'm not will you lock up?'

'Of course.'

'Then I'll see you on Tuesday. Take care and have a good weekend.'

'You too.'

Making her way out to where her car was parked, Caris found the sullen sky was pewter-grey with threatening black clouds looming on the horizon. But it had stopped raining, for which she gave thanks.

When she turned on the ignition the car engine, which normally started straight away, coughed, hesitated and died. Afraid that it wasn't going to start, she tried again and again, getting more and more flustered.

She was just about to give up and go for a taxi when it

finally sprang into life. Breathing a heartfelt sigh of relief, she put it into gear, let out the clutch and headed out of town.

Gracedieu, an extensive area of undulating parkland, was about seven or eight miles beyond Spitewinter and still relatively isolated despite the housing developments that were creeping ever closer.

Once Caris had left the main road, the rolling countryside was pretty, the quiet lanes pleasantly green and leafy with late spring.

Any other time she would have enjoyed the drive, but once again memories of Zander and the past were crowding in, filling her mind.

But she wouldn't dwell on the past. She wouldn't! Making a determined effort, she turned her thoughts to the afternoon ahead and the possible outcome.

Reaching South Lodge, she jumped out to open the tall, black wrought-iron gates with their gilded spikes and ornate hinges.

Presuming that Michael Grayson would be coming in the same way, she left them open. Sliding behind the wheel once more, she drove between stone pillars topped by crouching lions.

Gracedieu, though well-built and elegant, hadn't been lived in for a number of years and looked forlorn and deserted, its garden a wet tangle of weeds and shrubbery.

As her small car climbed the long, winding drive—now somewhat neglected and overgrown between glossy banks of budding rhododendrons—she thought how different it must once have looked, with enough gardening staff to care for it.

The manor house itself stood on fairly high ground but, screened by mature trees, it wasn't visible until she had rounded the last bend in the drive.

Though she had visited it several times in the past few weeks, it still had the 'wow' factor, and when she drew to a halt on the paved forecourt she paused to gaze her fill and imagine what it must be like to live there.

It was built of old mellow stone, a perfect example of a period manor house but in miniature. Its barley-sugar chimneys were creeper-entwined, many of its mullioned windows partially obscured by delicate trails of ivy, and its walls were festooned with scented honeysuckle and climbing roses, the early ones already in bloom.

It was utterly and completely charming. Had Caris been a multi-millionairess…

But she wasn't and never would be, she reminded herself wryly. She was just an ordinary woman with a job to do, so she'd better gather her wits and do it. She was a good hour early, so she would have ample time to take another look at all the relevant details before Michael Grayson got there.

Rather than staying in the car, she would go into the house and work in the kitchen. So long as she kept an eye on her watch, she could be outside in plenty of time to greet her client.

The air was heavy and oddly still, as if it were waiting with bated breath for the coming storm, but the rain was holding off and a few rays of weak sun were struggling to shine through a break in the clouds. She hoped it was a good omen.

Leaving her own set of keys in the ignition and her mac on the passenger seat, she picked up her briefcase and bag and made her way across the forecourt to the studded oak door.

Above the stone lintel of the door was a riot of sagging wisteria, and damp trails of it touched her neck as she selected one of the heavy, ornate keys from the big bunch that was weighing down her shoulder bag and let herself into the hall.

It had beautiful linenfold panelling, a big stone fireplace and polished oak floorboards, stippled now with light and shade. At one end was a minstrels' gallery, while at the other an oak staircase rose to a landing with long, tracery windows.

There were still some pieces of furniture scattered about and one or two mediocre paintings in heavy frames hung on the walls.

Crossing the hall, Caris opened the door to the large living-kitchen. With its black beams and inglenook fireplace, it was one of her favourite rooms. She always felt the past was present there, like some friendly ghost.

Towards the end of his long life, Gracedieu's previous owner had lived in this room and it was still fully furnished with an oak table and chairs, a period coffee table, two comfortable-looking armchairs, several sheepskin rugs and, incongruously, a modern divan bed on castors.

Huge cupboards held piles of household goods and linen, and a black stove stood in the fireplace with a stack of split logs on either side.

Crossing to the table, she put her belongings down and went to open a window a crack to let in some fresh air.

A riot of pale cream roses clambered damply up the outer wall and over the stone sill. Breathing in their haunting fragrance, she sat down at the table, opened her briefcase and started to go through the documents it contained— Or, rather, tried to.

The scent of the roses brought back vivid memories of Owl Lodge and the roses there, and instead of the printed pages all Caris could see was the past more real in her mind than the present…

Once she had agreed to stay the night at Owl Lodge, she had been beset by doubts.

It wasn't that she didn't trust Zander. The awful truth was, she wasn't at all sure she could trust herself.

Though she was certain that he wouldn't try to force her

in any way, he was a red-blooded man; suppose he turned up the heat? If he touched her, kissed her, would she be able to resist him?

But her youthful mistake had taught her a lot. After having been badly burnt once, surely she would have enough self-respect and pride, enough willpower, not to repeat the experience?

Or would she?

Wasn't it Oscar Wilde who had said, 'I can resist everything but temptation'? And Zander was temptation personified.

He and Karl weren't in the same league. They were both Lotharios, of course, but Karl had proved to be shallow, selfish and immature; only her own naivety had made him seem irresistible.

Zander, on the other hand, *was* irresistible. A mature, sophisticated, complex man with a depth, warmth and smouldering sex-appeal that never failed to ignite an answering spark.

Where he was concerned, she seemed to have little or no willpower. However, if she allowed herself no more erotic imaginings and kept a firm grip on her troubled emotions...

Sitting watching the doubts and worries flit across her face, Zander remarked with amusement in his tone, 'There's no need to look quite so apprehensive. I'm not about to leap on you and make mad, passionate love to you.'

Knowing he was making fun of her, she assured him a shade stiffly, 'I never thought you were.'

'Unless that's what you want, of course?'

'It isn't.'

'Then you've nothing to fear from me. Now, where were we before the lights went out?'

Relieved by the change of subject, she said, 'About to decide what to eat.'

'Of course. Though, now there's no electricity, sadly our options are reduced to what can be made on the stove.'

'But I still get to choose?'

'You bet!'

Wondering how he'd take the suggestion, she said, 'What I'd really like is something quite simple.'

Lifting an eyebrow, he waited.

For a few seconds she said nothing, her attention riveted by the way the red-gold firelight flickered on his face, turning it into an Aztec mask.

'Go on,' he urged. 'The suspense is unbearable.'

'If you have any bread…?'

Rising to his feet, he said, 'We certainly have. Ben's wife has left sourdough, milk and a good selection of fresh food in the fridge.'

He was back almost immediately with a nice-looking loaf, a breadboard, a knife and a plate, which he put on the low table.

'So what do you want to do with this bread?'

'I'd like to toast it on the stove and have it with lots of jelly and peanut butter, if you have any?'

'We sure do. Smooth or crunchy?'

'Oh, *crunchy*.'

'Have I already mentioned that you're a woman after my own heart?'

Watching him begin to slice the bread, she asked, 'Can I make the toast?'

'Do you want to?'

She nodded. 'Please. I've always enjoyed making toast on a fire.'

He pretended to consider. 'I could be chivalrous and insist on doing all the work myself, but I've often thought that male chivalry springs from a selfish desire to have all the fun, so go ahead.'

Putting the plate of bread on the hearth, he handed her a long-handled fork and watched as she knelt on the mat, favouring her damaged ankle, and started to toast the first piece.

When he returned from the kitchen carrying a tray loaded with more plates, knives, jam, a large jar of peanut butter, napkins and a fresh pot of coffee, she was just finishing a somewhat wonky pile of crisp, golden-brown slices.

He thought that with her deep-blue eyes sparkling, and her cheeks flushed from the heat, she made an enchanting picture.

As she leant forward, intent on her task, the lapels of her over-sized robe gaped a little, allowing a tantalizing glimpse of the soft curves of her breasts.

He looked at her and wanted her. Wanted her with every fibre of his being.

She put the last slice of toast on the plate. Glancing up unwarily, she met his eyes—eyes that had darkened to the deepest shade of jade—and read the smouldering passion in them.

Her own eyes widened and, transfixed, she found herself unable to look away as every nerve-ending in her body zinged into life and she burned with an answering passion.

The little stack of toast sliding off the plate broke the spell. Feeling oddly shaky, as if she had just found herself on the verge of some shattering experience, she dropped the toasting fork and began to re-stack the slices.

Watching her, he noticed how unsteady her hands were, and how that telltale pulse fluttered frantically at her throat.

His looks and background meant that usually women threw themselves at him, but something about this particular woman—a certain reserve, a hint of wariness—convinced him that no matter how much she wanted him she wouldn't make the first move.

Though it would be easy for him to seduce her.

Even as the thought went through his mind he knew that this time he wanted more than just an easy seduction. More than just a brief fling.

He wasn't sure as yet how *much* more, but already he recognised that their budding relationship mattered, and it was too important to risk spoiling it by rushing things. And taking her to bed now might rush things. Though in some ways he felt as if he had always known her, they had only met twenty-four hours ago.

Suppressing a sigh, he turned away to pull the table into a more convenient position. Then, his face schooled into a bland mask, he helped her to her feet and into a chair before passing her a plate, a knife and a napkin.

She was still feeling distinctly shaken when he sat down opposite and urged, 'Why don't you make a start while the toast's hot?'

Taking care to keep her eyes on what she was doing, she obeyed. His attitude was so relaxed, so matter-of-fact, that she found herself wondering if she could have possibly misread his earlier expression.

Yet she knew she hadn't. How he had looked at that moment seemed burnt into her brain, as was her own response to that look.

If he had made a move… But thankfully he hadn't.

Thankfully? Who was she trying to kid? When he had turned away, her overriding emotion had been disappointment.

But she must remember what had happened with Karl.

While she was sure Zander wasn't the uncaring swine that Karl had been, if she went to bed with him it was almost bound to end the same way.

And that meant with tears, regrets and her pride and self-respect in tatters. Bearing that in mind, she *must* steer clear of temptation.

CHAPTER FIVE

THEY finished the simple meal without another word being spoken. Still off-balance, Caris couldn't think of a single thing to say, and Zander seemed to be sunk in thought.

When their plates and mugs were empty, he loaded everything on to the tray and took it through to the kitchen.

Comfortably warm, Caris was just drifting into a doze when the latch clicked, announcing his return.

Rousing herself, she sat up straighter.

'Tired?' he asked.

About to admit that she was, she hesitated.

'If you want an early night…?'

The memory of her earlier erotic imaginings made her cheeks grow pink. She denied, 'No, no, I don't!'

Wondering at the vehemence of her reply, he queried, 'Sure?'

'Quite sure.' Involuntarily, she pulled the lapels of her robe together over her breasts.

Watching her, and speculating about the significance of that gesture, he suggested, 'Then suppose we have a nightcap?'

Having tossed a couple of logs into the stove, sending up a shower of bright sparks, he produced a bottle of Benedictine from a nearby cupboard and two balloon glasses.

When he had swirled a generous amount of the golden

liquid into the glasses, he handed her one before resuming his seat.

Still a little ill at ease, she stared fixedly into the flames while she sipped her drink. After a while, made even more sleepy by the alcohol, she was forced to stifle a yawn.

'Ready for bed now?' he enquired easily.

'Yes, I…I suppose so. Somehow it's been a long day,' she added.

'But on the whole an enjoyable one, I hope?'

'Very enjoyable.'

'I'm glad,' he said, and meant it.

Rising to his feet, he began to build up the fire. Catching her surprised glance, he explained, 'I usually keep the stove on.'

'Even in summer?'

'As I mentioned earlier we're fairly high up here, so even in summer the nights can be rather cool. Added to that, I sometimes have an early-morning dip in the lake…' He broke off laughing as she shuddered theatrically.

'Yes, it can be quite…refreshing,' he agreed. 'So when I've towelled off it's nice to have breakfast by the stove.'

'That part I can go along with wholeheartedly.'

'In that case, we're all set for tomorrow morning. Now we need to decide on something for you to wear to sleep in.'

'What about a spare pyjama top, if you have one?'

'Never wear the things. But I've just thought of something that might do.'

He went to the bedroom area and, sliding open the doors of the built-in storage space, returned with a navy-blue tee shirt. 'This will no doubt bury you, but it's the smallest thing I have.'

Accepting the soft cotton garment, she said, 'Thank you, that will be fine.'

'Then you can have first turn in the bathroom.'

Picking up an oil lamp and the kettle of water that had been heating on the stove, he led the way, remarking, 'I'm afraid there's not a lot of hot water, but there should be a spare toothbrush and anything else you may need in the cupboard.'

He placed the kettle on the floor and the lamp on a shelf, where it cast strange shadows, and then he went, closing the door behind him.

When she had cleaned her teeth, she poured half the hot water into the sink, steaming up the mirror, and reluctantly took off her robe.

The air felt decidedly chill and she washed quickly, shivering a little, pulling on the tee shirt. It was thigh-length and the shoulders were much too wide, but it felt easy and comfortable, and it was oddly exciting to be wearing something that Zander had worn.

Having no wish to look seductive—in fact, quite the opposite—she brushed her long silky hair and fastened it into a single thick braid.

Then, very conscious of her bare legs, she pulled on the robe once more before returning to the warmth of the living room as fast as her ankle would allow.

Glancing up, Zander asked, 'Manage all right?'

'Yes, thanks. I've left you half the hot water.'

'Oh generous woman! In that case I'll go and make use of it. By the way, there's no need to wait for me. If you want to go to bed, feel free.'

But, shying away from the thought of the coming night, she went back to her chair by the stove and stretched her slim bare feet to the blaze.

While she had been gone, Zander had put a pillow and a couple of blankets on the couch, ready for use.

But it was ridiculous! she realized belatedly. The couch

was far too short for a man of his height. It would make more sense for her to sleep on it.

Had she been a different sort of woman, they could have shared the bed. But, while casual sex might work for some, she had never thought it was for her. Her one disastrous brush with passion had only served to confirm that.

Even so, while a pool of molten heat began to form in the pit of her stomach, she found herself imagining what it would like to lie in his arms, to have him kiss her while those long-fingered hands touched her intimately...

'Still up?'

She jumped a mile as Zander resumed his chair.

'I thought you were ready for bed?'

Hoping he would put her high colour down to the warmth of the fire, she said, 'The trip to the bathroom woke me up.'

He smiled at her. 'In that case, I'll join you by the fire for a while...'

Caris had heard no sound, but something—a kind of awareness that she was no longer alone—brought her back to the present with a start.

While she had been sitting in Gracedieu's kitchen immersed in the past the sky had turned as black as night. The kitchen was in semi-darkness as she looked up, Zander's smiling face still filling her mind.

Dressed in smart casuals, he was standing there in the gloom as though her thoughts had conjured him up. His hair was still the colour of ripe corn, and his handsome face was just as she remembered, but he wasn't smiling. In fact, she had never seen his expression so grim and set.

For an instant shock seemed to stop her heart. Then, unable to believe what her eyes were telling her, she blinked to clear her vision.

But he continued to stand there staring at her.

For what seemed an age she simply gaped at him, unable to take it in, more than half-convinced he was simply an hallucination.

Then, her heart racing, she croaked, 'Zander?'

Still he didn't speak. Rising to her feet, she said through stiff lips, 'What are you doing here?'

His attractive voice brusque, he answered, 'Waiting to see over the manor.'

Still her brain refused to kick into action. 'See over the manor…?' she echoed.

Taking in her neat appearance—the coiled hair, the leather court-shoes, the businesslike suit and briefcase—he said, 'Surely you're here to represent Carlton Lees estate agency?'

'Well, yes,' she agreed weakly. 'But my appointment was with a Mr Grayson.'

'I'm here in his place.'

'Here in his place?' she echoed. Half-shaking her head, she said, 'You don't mean you work for him?'

'No. He works for me. You see, while he's the nominal head of Grayson Holdings, I own it.'

So it was Zander who was interested in buying Gracedieu. If only she had known that, wild horses wouldn't have dragged her here.

'How did you know where to find me?' The moment the words were out, she realized what a foolish question it had been and felt her colour rise.

He gave no quarter. 'I was expecting you to be somewhere in the vicinity, and I could hardly miss the car parked outside,' he replied sardonically.

There was something in his manner, a kind of grim satisfaction, that made her wonder: had he known exactly who would be representing Carlton Lees?

While she had been knocked sideways to see him, he didn't

seem at all surprised to see her. Was it simply that he was better at hiding his feelings? Or was it possible that he had planned this meeting?

No, why should he have?

When they had parted three years ago there had been distrust and animosity on both sides, and nothing had happened to change that.

In any case he couldn't have known she was living in England. No one knew. And, if he'd thought about it at all, he would have been expecting her to follow a career in law, not be working as an estate agent. So it had to be just a devastating coincidence.

Becoming aware that he was standing quietly waiting, his eyes on her face, she struggled to pull herself together. No matter how difficult she found the situation, she still had a job to do.

Trying for a businesslike manner, she asked, 'I presume you would like to look over the house first before you see the estate and the cottages?'

'It seems the logical way to do it,' he said, making her feel a complete fool for asking.

Flustered, she went on, 'It's quite dark in here, though I'm afraid I didn't think to bring a torch and the electricity's been turned off.'

'No electricity, dear me!'

As she gritted her teeth, annoyed that he was making fun of her, he drawled, 'Oh well, I dare say we'll manage somehow.'

Wanting desperately to turn and run, but feeling forced to go through with the viewing, she took a steadying breath. Outwardly calm and collected in spite of the emotional turmoil that raged inside, she turned to lead the way.

'Then if you'd like to follow me...?'

It sounded ridiculously pompous and, realizing she was

making things worse, she felt her face grow hot; she was pleased that the shadows hid her embarrassment.

Caris paused to open the door when a cool hand touched her burning cheek, making her jump convulsively. She took an involuntary step backwards and, her heart racing, found herself trapped in the angle between the door and wall.

Zander was even taller than she remembered, his shoulders broader, his closeness overpowering as he stood blocking her escape route.

His fingers lingering lightly on her cheek, he commented softly, 'So you still blush… Seeing you look so businesslike and composed made me wonder.'

Finding it almost impossible to draw air into her lungs, she stood still as any statue.

Innocently, he asked, 'Something wrong?'

'No, nothing,' she lied breathlessly.

'That's good.'

When he removed his hand she hurried to make her escape into the hall, with a gasp of relief she feared was audible.

But at once he was with her, much too big, much too male, and she felt half-suffocated by his nearness.

'Let me see, there are how many rooms?' he queried casually.

Convinced that he already knew quite well how many rooms there were, she drew a deep, steadying breath and said, 'Twenty-three. Downstairs, apart from the hall, there are two good-sized reception rooms, the living-kitchen you've already seen, a formal living-room, a breakfast room, a dining room, a study-cum-library and two bathrooms. Upstairs there are eight bedrooms, three dressing rooms and two bathrooms.

'The attics were once the servants' quarters, but what used to be a large stable block has been converted into garages with modern accommodation above it for the household staff.'

'Know the dimensions?'

'Certainly...' In her most businesslike manner, she reeled off the information.

'How very brisk and efficient,' he murmured with mock admiration.

'How very nice of you to say so,' she responded sweetly.

He gave her a sharp glance and said no more.

She was just congratulating herself on keeping her cool when a flash of lightning followed by a loud clap of thunder made her flinch; rain began to beat against the mullioned windows.

As they moved through the low-ceilinged rooms, the light was so bad that they could hardly see where they were going.

From time to time, whether intentionally or accidentally, Zander's arm brushed hers. Whenever they paused he seemed able to herd her into a corner so that she felt confined, trapped.

Indicating the dark shapes shrouded in dust sheets, he queried, 'Why is there still furniture here?'

'The beneficiary lives in Australia,' Caris explained. 'As he hates flying, he didn't want to make the trip over to England, so he decided to have the most valuable things removed for auction. As he's hoping for a quick sale, he left everything else in situ for the new owner to dispose of as he or she wished.'

'Then he's not likely to change his mind about selling?' Zander asked.

'No. He has no interest whatsoever in the house or the estate. All he cares about is getting his money as quickly as possible.'

'Does that mean he might be willing to drop the price?'

'He won't need to,' she said with certainty. 'There's already a lot of interest in the property, and several people waiting to view.'

'And are all your prospective clients willing to purchase the entire estate as it stands?' Zander asked shrewdly.

He had unerringly put his finger on the main stumbling block. With such an enormous amount of money involved, at least two of the people on her list only wanted to buy the manor itself.

The beneficiary, whilst wanting to get rid of the entire estate, didn't mind if the land and the cottages were sold off piecemeal.

But Caris thought it would be a great pity, and was hoping to find a buyer who could and would keep the estate together.

'So are they?' Zander pressed.

'Are you?' she countered.

'To my mind, breaking up the estate would be like breaking up a perfect, irreplaceable diamond.'

'That's exactly how I feel.'

The moment the words were out she could have bitten her tongue. As he clearly had no very friendly feelings towards her, she should have kept her sentiments to herself.

A further disturbing thought struck her: would the fact that she owned the agency make any difference to his decision whether or not to buy Gracedieu?

No, surely not? If he was really interested in the place, it was unlikely that he would allow personal considerations to influence him.

And she certainly couldn't accuse him of lack of interest, she thought impatiently; he lingered to examine everything with a calculated deliberation that began to fray her nerves.

The first of the downstairs bathrooms had an old claw-footed bath and obsolete fittings and didn't appear to have been used for years.

The one next door to the kitchen, however, had been especially adapted to meet a disabled person's needs, and was quite up to date. Only the original heavy oak door had been retained, its ornate key still in the lock.

Reaching out a hand, Zander experimentally turned one of the gleaming taps and water splashed into the wash-basin.

The silence was becoming oppressive, and when he remarked on the walk-in bath and shower she was glad to explain that the previous owner had been a very old man.

'It seems he was a bit of a recluse and extremely independent. The only person he would allow in the house was a woman from the village, who did his cleaning and his shopping.

'Though his health was starting to fail, he wanted to stay in the home he loved without any outside "interference", so when he could no longer manage the stairs he decided to have a wet-room put in and turn the kitchen into a kind of bedsit.'

'I wondered what a bed was doing in there,' Zander remarked, adding, 'And was he able to? Stay in his own home, I mean?'

'Yes, apparently he managed quite well for a while,' Caris answered as she led the way across the hall and began to climb the stairs. 'But last winter he caught pneumonia and died in hospital at the age of ninety-eight.'

Apart from their footsteps on the oak boards, the only sound was that of the storm raging outside. She was very aware of them being so alone, so isolated, cut off from the rest of the world.

She had hoped that Zander would take a more or less cursory walk through the upstairs rooms, but in spite of the chill air he seemed inclined to linger.

Growing restive, she made a determined attempt to speed things up. But, refusing to be hurried, he took his time.

When finally the tour was over and he allowed himself to be led down the servants' stairs and back to the kitchen, Caris breathed a sigh of relief.

She couldn't wait to get away.

Pausing only to close and latch the window she had opened earlier, she gathered up her belongings and said crisply, 'Well, now you've seen over the house, would you like to take a look at the garage block?'

Prowling round the kitchen, peering into drawers and cupboards, he shook his head dismissively. 'The garage block isn't important; it can wait.'

'Then shall we move on?'

'Move on?'

'I presume you want to take a tour of the estate?'

'In this weather?' His tone held incredulity.

As though to add weight to his objections, a particularly fierce gust of wind and rain beat against the casements.

'Well, if you'd prefer to leave it for another day?'

'I wouldn't,' he said categorically.

Momentarily at a loss, she asked, 'Then what do you suggest we do?'

'Stay here and wait until the storm's over.'

Seized by a sudden panic, she cried, 'Oh no, I really can't!'

He raised a well-defined brow. 'Does that mean you want to call the whole thing off?'

'No, certainly not,' she denied hastily. 'But, as the weather's so bad, instead of wasting both your time and mine surely it would be preferable to make other arrangements to see over the estate?'

'It may be months before I'm back in this country; though I felt that Gracedieu might exactly suit my needs, there are other possible places on the market. But it's up to you,' he ended blandly.

She hesitated, more than reluctant to remain here in his company while he watched her in silence, a glint in his eye.

Finally, knowing that he held the whip hand, she agreed, 'Then, of course I'll stay.'

His little smile acknowledging that he knew it too, he said, 'I thought you might.'

'For a while at least,' she qualified, unwilling to be browbeaten.

He gave her a quick glance but said no more.

It had been a terrible shock to find she was dealing with Zander, but now circumstances were turning the whole thing into an absolute nightmare.

Seeing the involuntary shiver that ran through her, he enquired solicitously, 'Cold? Don't worry; I'll soon get the stove going.'

Not wanting him to get too settled, she objected, 'But surely you won't be able to. I mean…won't everything be damp?'

'We'll see.'

While she hovered unhappily, he unearthed some kindling from a nearby log-basket, remarking with a prosaic tone, 'This seems dry enough.'

She could see no sign of any matches, and she was just breathing a sigh of relief when he found a box.

He soon coaxed the kindling into life and it took only a second or two for a few small, carefully placed pieces of wood to catch fire. They were followed by a selection of split logs, and in a very short space of time the leaping flames were providing some much-needed light and warmth.

Pulling the armchairs closer to the blaze, he suggested, 'Why don't you come and sit down where it's warm?' His tone was neutral, neither friendly nor unfriendly.

Seeing nothing else for it, she reluctantly joined him by the fire.

As soon as she was seated, Zander sat down in the chair opposite and, leaning back, stretched his long legs towards the blaze and crossed his ankles.

He appeared to be quite comfortable, relaxed, but she could

sense an underlying tension that told a different story, and the green eyes fixed on her were clouded with sombre thoughts.

Though she tried her hardest not to look in his direction, her furtive gaze was drawn irresistibly to his face.

He was as handsome as ever, those long, heavy-lidded eyes just as fascinating, while above a fine black polo-necked sweater his hair looked even fairer than she remembered.

Yes, he was the same, yet not the same. The carefree young man she had known was gone. Now he appeared older and there were lines of strain beside his mouth that hadn't been there three years ago.

She found herself wondering what had caused them.

There was so much between them that had been left unsaid. With mingled feelings of trepidation and inevitability, Caris waited for him to speak, to bring up the past. To ask the question she was dreading having to answer.

But the seconds ticked away and still he said nothing, merely watched her.

Totally unnerved by that brooding scrutiny, she sought for a safe topic of conversation. But the silence stretched between them, dangerous as a minefield, and try as she might she could think of nothing to say or any way to defuse the situation.

All at once the storm raging outside and the tension inside took her back to Owl Lodge and that first night when, reluctant to go to bed, she and Zander had been sitting by the fire in silence...

The tension, a sexual one, had been almost tangible until the storm that had been threatening all evening finally broke, snapping like an overstretched rubber band.

Rain began to drum on the roof and beat against the windows, while drops falling down the chimney hissed as they hit the burning logs.

Jumping to his feet, Zander exclaimed, 'Hell! I forgot to close the car roof.'

Pulling on his damp shoes and an oilskin that hung behind the door, he hurried out into the darkness.

He returned quite quickly, the oilskin gleaming in the lamplight, his hair darkened by the wet drops of rain running down his face.

'Everything all right?' she asked,

'Not too bad, considering. Though it's a bit wild out there.'

Hanging up the oilskin, he fetched a towel to rub his hair and dry his face before resuming his seat by the fire and leaning back at his ease, his eyes half-closed.

With his thick, curly lashes almost brushing his hard cheeks, his hair slightly rumpled, his lips a little parted and a golden stubble adorning his chin, he looked incredibly sexy.

In spite of all her efforts to stay unmoved, Caris's breathing grew laboured and her pulse-rate quickened as she imagined those beautiful, sculptured lips touching hers...

'Penny for them.'

Flustered by the intent way he was studying her face, she found herself blushing furiously.

'Sorry,' he apologized, proving he didn't lack sensitivity. 'I didn't mean to stare. But you looked so...' He broke off.

Knowing that her nose was shiny and the thick braid hanging over one shoulder must look schoolgirlish to a sophisticated man like Zander, she said, 'I imagine I look an absolute fright.'

He shook his head. 'I wouldn't say that.'

'Then what *would* you say?' she asked, without really thinking.

Smiling, he told her, 'That you look utterly enchanting, seductive, sweet and sensuous, like a woman who's longing to be made love to...'

Panic bringing her to her feet, she said jerkily, 'I'm start-

ing to feel really tired now, so I think it would be better if I
went to bed after all…'

Realizing that she was babbling, she broke off abruptly,
biting her lip.

He rose too, his face straight, his eyes devilishly amused.
He queried, 'Alone?'

'Alone!' she croaked.

'Of course—if you're *sure* that's what you want?'

'Yes, I'm sure. But, as I'm nowhere near as tall as you, it
would make more sense for me to sleep on the couch.'

'I won't hear of it.'

'But I *want* you to have the bed,' she insisted. 'Otherwise
I'd feel guilty.'

He shook his head decidedly. 'The only way I'm prepared
to sleep in the bed is if you want to share it with me.'

Seeing on her expressive face the return of her previous
panic, he said carefully, 'I meant platonically. I'm not trying
to take advantage of the situation, and I'm noted for my self-
control.'

It was her own self-control she didn't trust, rather than his,
but she could hardly tell him that.

'So, as soon as I've seen you safely tucked in, I'll retire to
my couch.'

With a slight sigh, he added, 'Though I frankly admit that
I want you more than I've ever wanted any other woman…'

Somehow she found her voice. Struggling to sound both
amused and dismissive, she said, 'I bet you say that to any
girl who comes along.'

'I won't deny there have been other women, but the way I
feel about you is different, unprecedented. The instant I set
eyes on you, you affected me strangely, touched my heart…'

He took a step forward, his voice low and intense. He murmured, 'Though I didn't really know you at all, I felt as if I
did. As if, somehow, I'd always known you.'

I know you too, she thought. *I know you as if you were part of me.*

But he was going on. 'You delight me, enchant me, and I've thought of little else but taking you in my arms and making love with you...'

Gently he laid the flat of his hand against her cheek, and with a little murmur she turned her mouth into his palm. His other hand came up to cup her face and then his mouth was moving against hers.

Their first kiss, a kiss they had both been waiting so long for, was a slow and gentle brushing of lips, but it said far more than either of them could have put into words at that moment.

When he finally drew back, she was flushed and euphoric, and a glance at his face showed that everything she was feeling, he was feeling too.

The realization was overwhelming, and it sent a charge like electricity running through her. Lips a little parted, she swayed towards him.

With a hand at the back of her head, he drew that lovely face to his. Then his mouth was on hers once more, tasting, enjoying, lingering seductively, as though he could happily spend the rest of his life just kissing her.

The quiet joy of it, the warmth and sense of belonging, the sweetness and passion, wound silken ribbons of need around her heart.

Clearly he felt the same, because the romance and chasteness of his previous kisses flared into desire and sensuality.

Every nerve-ending in her body came to life and her skin waited, longing for his touch, the blood running hot beneath it.

Then his hands were inside her robe, following the elegant line of her spine, the dip of her narrow waist and the flair of her hips, before they moved upwards to caress her breasts through the soft cotton of the tee shirt she was wearing.

She sighed and her head fell back, surrendering the long, elegant line of her throat to his lips...

While he kissed her, he unfastened the robe and slipped it off her shoulders, letting it fall to the floor; an instant later, the tee shirt followed it. Swinging her up in his arms, he laid her gently on the couch.

She was the loveliest thing he'd ever seen, with beautifully shaped breasts, a small waist, rounded hips and long, slender limbs. Her skin was flawless, smooth as satin and tempting to touch.

The fire-glow turned her slender figure to the purest gold, and when he did finally touch her he felt like King Midas.

Until that moment he hadn't realized just how much he had to give, just how much he *wanted* to give this woman: everything he was, everything he had, everything he felt.

Sitting on the edge of the couch, he ran his hands over her body as though it was rare and precious, something he would never get tired of exploring.

Touch was cited as the most powerful of the senses, certainly the most seductive; as he stroked and caressed her, the last of her worries and concerns melted away and with a sigh her heavy lids drifted shut.

Her obvious enjoyment fuelling his, he began to use his lips, mouth and tongue to find new ways to heighten her pleasure, while the taste and scent of her made him feel almost light-headed.

His skilled fingers teasing one dusky-pink nipple, he took the other into his mouth and stroked the sensitive tip with his tongue before starting to suckle sweetly.

She gave a throaty gasp and her whole body jerked convulsively as a shock of unaccustomed delight ran through her.

While her breasts blossomed at his touch, his free hand travelled to the smooth skin of her inner thighs. When his long fingers began to explore the slick warmth with delicate precision, making little incoherent sounds deep in her throat, she tried to push him away.

He drew back immediately. Taking a deep breath, he asked, 'Is that a no? If it is, say so at once.'

'No...' she breathed.

Disappointment sharp as shards of jagged glass slashed at him. Getting to his feet, he struggled hard to regain his self-control.

As he reached for her robe, she opened her eyes and caught at his hand. 'I meant no—it isn't a "no".'

'It *isn't* a no?' he repeated. 'So what is it?'

'It's a yes please.'

'Then why did you push me away?'

'It was so... So...'

'You didn't like what I was doing to you?'

'Yes, yes, I did. It was wonderful.'

Letting go of his hand, she pushed herself up into a sitting position before going on in a rush, 'But so intense I just didn't think I could stand any more at that minute.'

His smile held both tenderness and relief. 'Well, if that's all, we can take things a tad slower...'

CHAPTER SIX

HE WAS bending his fair head to kiss her when his face clouded and in soft frustration he exclaimed, 'Oh hell!'

All at once on his wavelength, and impatient now, she said quickly, 'It's all right. For medical reasons I'm on the pill.'

He nodded and kissed her, before saying teasingly, 'Now, let's see, where were we exactly?'

Sounding breathless even to herself, she said, 'About to take things a little slower.'

'So where would you like to start?'

Though still a little shy, she wanted to look at him, to see his body.

'You're still wearing your robe,' she pointed out.

'Well, that can soon be remedied.' He untied the belt and tossed the robe aside.

Standing before her, tall, straight and naked, he enquired, 'Better?'

But her mouth had gone dry and she could only gaze at him speechlessly.

He was *gorgeous*, with wide shoulders, a trim waist, narrow hips, and strong, straight limbs. Fit and toned, without being muscle-bound, he carried not an ounce of spare flesh.

Both his lower arms and his calves were covered with a fine scattering of short golden hair, but his broad chest was smooth and his clear, tanned skin held the gleam of health.

Though normally the least vain of men, seeing the awe and pleasure she was feeling register on her face made him feel like Suleiman the Magnificent.

'Seen enough?' he teased.

She blinked, as though coming out of a dream, and looked up.

When he smiled at her, she smiled back, alluring as Lorelei. But he had promised to take things slowly, he warned himself.

Stooping, he kissed her gently before sitting down beside her and taking her in his arms.

For a while, as the storm continued to rage outside, they just kissed, each anticipating all the delight still to come; then, growing impatient, she nipped his bottom lip provocatively.

In response he deepened the kiss and, gathering her into his arms, carried her over to the bed. When she was settled beneath the lightweight duvet, he slipped in beside her.

Starting where he had left off, he proceeded to pleasure her, whispering how sweet and innocently lovely she was, how desirable, how very much he wanted her.

With a little murmur she drew him to her, her body welcoming his smoothly, ecstatically, as though it had been waiting a lifetime for just this moment.

For a while after that first long, slow thrust, he simply lay, enjoying the feeling of her slender body beneath his.

Filled with him, and eager for more, she moved her hips in an invitation as old as Eve. But when he finally moved there was no urgency; the pace was leisurely, luxurious, and they made love in a silence which only served to increase all the delicious sensations she was experiencing.

Even when the momentum increased, it still seemed tantalizingly slow and erotic, until finally and together they reached the dazzling heights of physical pleasure before drifting back to earth.

She had never known anything like this before, Caris thought with wonder. Their love-making had proved to be a joyful and *complete* experience.

They had met and joined on every level—physical, mental and emotional. There were no words to describe such bliss, a bliss that encompassed both body and soul.

Her eyes closed, lying quietly fulfilled, she cradled Zander's fair head against her breast with an almost maternal tenderness.

After a while he raised his head and, lifting himself away, he kissed her. 'You're very quiet. Are you all right?'

She opened her eyes and smiled up at him, and in the faint glow from the stove and the dying lamp he read all he needed to know in her face—even before she answered with a slight chuckle, 'Euphoric!'

Human and male enough to feel a touch of triumph mingle with the satisfaction and happiness he was already feeling, he kissed her again. Then, brushing a strand of dark hair away from her cheek, he turned onto his back and gathered her close. She fell asleep almost immediately.

Quietly content, he lay for a while breathing in the scent of her hair and enjoying the feel of her cradled in his arms.

When he had said that this was different, unprecedented, he'd been speaking the exact truth. No woman—and he was no stranger to women—had ever made him feel this way or given him more pleasure

His last thought before he too fell asleep was that she was everything he could have hoped for and more, and he owed fate a big debt of gratitude for the chance meeting that had thrown them together.

Caris awoke to find the storm had passed in the night and the pale light of a quiet dawn was creeping beneath the curtains and filling the cabin.

She was stretched on her back. Zander was still sleeping, lying on his side, one arm across her midriff. In the unaccustomed silence, she could hear his quiet, even breathing.

Last night had been wonderful. She hadn't known lovemaking could be like that. With Karl it had always proved to be disappointing, and at first she had blamed herself and her own lack of experience.

But after he had left her and moved on she had heard one of the other girls, a philosophy student, remark to her companion, 'Oh, Karl was gorgeous and *seemed* exciting until I got to know him. Then I discovered that he was not only boring but selfish and shallow and uncaring, without a clue how to turn a woman on.'

'I know exactly what you mean,' her fellow student had agreed. 'Apart from his looks, he was a dead loss. His idea of foreplay—had he ever heard of such a thing—would probably have been to say, "Brace yourself, sweetie".'

The two girls had laughed together before the second one had added half-jokingly, 'Perhaps all he needs to change him is the love of a good woman.'

'I'd be sorry for any woman who fell in love with him! In my opinion he's emotionally bankrupt, incapable of loving anyone other than himself.'

It had been a damning indictment, yet over the years the brief and ill-advised affair had continued to shame and haunt her.

And now, after all her warnings to herself, she had ended up in another Lothario's bed.

She should be full of shame and regrets, castigating herself for allowing it to happen, but all she could feel was an intense, overriding joy...

A tingle of awareness made her turn her head; sure enough, Zander was awake. She could see his green eyes gleaming through their thick curtain of dark-blond lashes.

He smiled at her and, using the arm draped over her waist, turned her to face him. 'Good morning.'

Returning his smile a little shyly, she answered, 'Good morning.'

Reaching out a hand, he stroked her cheek. 'Did I remember to tell you how beautiful you are?'

His words, and the tenderness of the gesture, sent her floating up to cloud nine.

But she did her best to keep her feet on the ground and objected, 'I'm not really beautiful, merely average. And no one can look beautiful at this time in the morning.'

'Wrong on both counts. When I first walked into your office, when I looked at you over a candlelit dinner table, when you sat in the sun-drenched kitchen at Hallgarth, your beauty took my breath away. And this morning it still does.'

'Is this a line you shoot any woman who ends up in your bed?'

'Only if her face is like a flower, she has hair as silky-dark as night and eyes the deep, pure blue of a summer dusk just before the fireflies come out. Only if she's warm and sweet and feminine and a delight to make love to...'

Watching her cheeks turn pink, he asked teasingly, 'Am I waxing too lyrical for you? Would you prefer a more practical approach at this time of the day?'

Gathering herself, she suggested lightly, 'Try me and see.'

Running lean fingers over his stubbly chin, he pretended to consider. Then with a straight face he enquired, 'What would you say to an early-morning swim together? At this hour we'd have the lake to ourselves, so you wouldn't need a costume.'

She shuddered. 'I *do* hope you're joking?'

'As a matter of fact, I am. To tell you the truth I had some other activity in mind that should be even more pleasurable...'

'Oh?' She raised an eyebrow at him.

'And it doesn't even necessitate getting out of bed,' he added coaxingly.

'Now, what can that be?' she wondered aloud.

'Allow me to show you.'

If last night's love-making had been threaded with poetry and a kind of awe, in the early morning it proved to be just as thrilling and even more erotic.

His hand on the duvet, he enquired, 'Warm enough?'

'Why do you ask?'

'Because I'd very much like to be able to look at you while I make love to you, to watch your reactions and see how I make you feel.'

His words sent a little quiver running through her. 'Well?'

'Yes, I'm warm enough.'

Her whispered response earned her a kiss, an affectionate kiss, which in a moment became a kiss of mutual desire. A kiss full of sizzling lust.

Pushing the duvet down, he turned her onto her back and let his hand explore her slender body, watching her nipples firm at his touch, her stomach clench, the shiver that ran through her when he reached the smooth skin of her inner thighs.

But, though she was ready and eager, and his need for her was as explosive as a lightning strike, he still made himself take it slowly.

Refusing to hurry, his mouth enjoyed and pleasured those waiting nipples before he moved up to the long sweep of her neck and let his lips linger there.

Then, looking deeply into her eyes, he fitted himself into the waiting cradle of her hips, two bodies perfectly designed to become one.

Still holding her gaze, he began to move. He heard her breathing quicken, saw the flush of excitement on her cheeks, the dazed pleasure in her eyes, and knew without a doubt that it was as good for her as it was for him.

Neither of them spoke. There was no need for words as in perfect union they tumbled into a whirlpool of sensation.

When at last their breathing and heartbeat slowed to a more normal pace, he lifted himself away; drawing her close, he settled her head comfortably on his shoulder.

Utterly content, she snuggled against him and drifted off to sleep once more.

The next time Caris opened her eyes the grey light of dawn had been replaced by bright sunshine, and she was alone in the bed. An enticing smell of fresh coffee hung in the air and the stove was burning brightly but there was no sign of Zander.

She stretched luxuriously, and for a moment lay savouring the happiness that filled her while she thought of all the delight another day spent in his company would hold.

Suddenly she couldn't wait to see him, to go into his arms and lift her face for his kiss.

She was halfway out of bed when she heard voices coming from the direction of the kitchen. One she recognized as Zander's, the other was a man's voice she had never heard before.

Afraid that the owner of the strange voice might be coming in, she got back into bed and hastily pulled up the duvet to cover her nakedness. But when the kitchen door opened, only Zander appeared.

He was dressed in light, casual trousers and a mulberry-coloured shirt, open at the neck, both of which had seen better days. His hair was damp and tousled as if he'd hastily rubbed it dry and left it, but somehow he still managed to look self-assured and coolly elegant.

'So you're awake.' He came over to the bed and, sitting on the edge, gave her a light, fleeting kiss.

Deciding to tease him, she grumbled, 'That showed a distinct lack of enthusiasm.'

He ran his fingers over his unshaven chin. 'I realized I shouldn't be inflicting this on you.'

'I admit you look a bit like a caveman, but you can't use that as an excuse. I quite like cavemen, and I like stubble.'

'Do you really?' he asked interestedly. 'In that case...' Pulling down the duvet, he began to nuzzle his face against her breasts.

The rasp of the stubble over her sensitive nipples was so unbearably erotic that she gave a stifled squeak and tried to push him away.

But, catching her wrists, he kept her captive while he began to rove over her entire body, only giving in to her laughing and breathless pleas to stop when she began to gasp, 'I'm sorry... I'm sorry... I didn't mean it.'

'What didn't you mean?' he asked sternly.

'I didn't mean it about the lack of enthusiasm.'

Releasing her wrists, he said severely, 'I should hope not. But if you still have any doubts that need dispelling we could always spend the day in bed.'

She was about to deny that she still had doubts when he went on with a gleam in his eye, 'In fact, I don't see any reason why we shouldn't spend the day in bed anyway.'

Hastily, she told him, 'Well, *I* do.'

'I hope this lack of enthusiasm on your part is only temporary?'

'It's just that it's such a lovely day, and I'd like to see a little more of Square Lake before we start back.'

He sighed. 'Well, if I have to wait until tonight, at least give me a kiss to be going on with.'

Lifting her face, she offered him her mouth.

When he'd finally and reluctantly freed her lips, she remarked, 'Earlier I thought I heard voices.'

'Yes, that would be Ben. He's just gone. I got hold of him first thing, and the good news is he's managed to fix the generator. Which means we can both have a shower.'

Glancing at his damp hair, she observed, 'You look as if you've already had yours.'

He shook his head. 'When there's only cold water, I prefer the lake.'

She shuddered.

He grinned. 'However, I can certainly use a hot shower now. But I suggest that you go first while I start to fix breakfast. Oh, by the way, your clothes are dry.'

'That's great.'

'I'm not so sure.' He gave her a lascivious grin. 'If they hadn't been, we might have been forced to spend the day in bed. Still, as you remarked, it's lovely weather, so we'll make the most of it before we go back to civilization.'

Caris had liked Hallgarth and she had enjoyed her short stay there. But Square Lake had proved to be an idyllic spot, an enchanted world, and she felt a pang of regret that they would be leaving today.

Zander, who had gone to fetch her robe, watched as she swung her feet to the floor and gingerly tested her ankle.

'How does it seem?' he enquired.

'Much less painful today.'

'Even so, it would pay to go carefully for another day or two.'

'I expect you're right, though I would have loved to take a walk along the lake-shore before we go.'

Hearing the longing in her voice, he knew she had fallen under the spell of the place in much the same way as he himself had.

'Never mind,' he said consolingly. 'We can always put a lake-shore walk on the list of things to do when your ankle's fully mended.'

Before her ankle was fully mended, it was odds on that *she* would be back at work and *he* would be halfway round the world.

But she mustn't be ungrateful. Whatever fate had in store, there was still today to spend in his company. And she dared not think more than one day at a time; it seemed like tempting fate.

He helped her into the robe and as she began to fasten it made to slip his hand inside, but she playfully slapped it away. 'I need a shower, and you promised me breakfast.'

Sighing, he agreed. 'So I did. Ah, well...'

With a come-hither glance, she suggested demurely, 'Of course it might save time, not to mention water, if we showered together.'

He picked her up in his arms and kissed her. 'As I've said before, you're a woman after my own heart.'

When they stood together beneath the flow of hot water, Zander filled his palms with shower gel and ran his hands over her wet body with an erotic but leisurely enjoyment.

She longed to do the same to him, but a certain shyness held her back.

As though reading her thoughts, he said a little huskily, 'Touch me if you want to.'

At first her hands were tentative; then when she saw that he was taking pleasure in her touch they grew bolder.

She stroked her palms over his shoulders, his muscular upper arms and broad chest, her fingers revelling in the feel of the smooth skin and the small nipples.

Working her way downwards, she reached the nest of golden curls nestling at the base of his flat stomach and, greatly daring, explored further.

She heard the breath hiss through his teeth and realized with a thrill of excitement that she had the same power over him as he had over her.

Before she could put it to use, however, his fingers closed around her wrist. 'I hope you know what you're doing?'

'Doing?' she echoed innocently.

'Yes, doing.'

Glancing up at him through long lashes, she said plaintively, 'But I thought you were enjoying it.'

He bent to kiss her. 'So I was, you little minx. But we could have some shared enjoyment.'

'We had some shared enjoyment earlier,' she pointed out sedately. 'In fact I don't know how you…'

Catching sight of the amusement in his eyes, she broke off in confusion.

He laughed. 'Being this close to you when you have no clothes on energizes me.'

'Is that what you call it?'

'In polite company. But, whatever you care to call it, shared enjoyment has got to be better.'

Backing her against the wall of the shower, he proceeded to prove it.

Afterwards he dried her thoroughly from head to toe, kissing every inch of her skin as he did so and ensuring that she ended up warm and glowing with contentment and pleasure.

Her things had been placed ready on the stool, and while he towelled himself she began to pull them on.

Noticing her grimace, he asked, 'Something wrong?'

'No, not really. It's just that I would have preferred a change of clothing.'

'Then you won't like what I have in mind.'

'What have you in mind?'

'I was about to suggest that to give you more chance to look around we stayed here again tonight and went back tomorrow morning.'

Her heart leapt; eager to prolong their idyll, she said, 'I suppose I could always do some laundry before I go to bed.'

He smiled. 'Have I mentioned that you're a woman in a million?'

'Not for at least five minutes.'

'Then I must tell you more often.' With a snatched kiss, he took himself off to make breakfast.

When she had finished drying her hair she swept it up into a bouncy ponytail before making her way onto the front porch.

The air was cool and as sparkling as iced champagne. From a cloudless sky the deep, dark blue of lapis lazuli, sun was pouring down, golden as honey, making myriad raindrops glitter like diamonds on the trees and reeds.

Everywhere was beautiful, still and peaceful. The mirror-calm water reflected the wooded shoreline and rocky promontories, while in the distance the blue sunlit mountains looked serene and enchanted.

Out on the water a rowing boat rode idly while its occupant fished, and closer at hand a bright-red canoe went skimming past.

Caris was watching a dabble of ducks splash and tip their tails in the air as they searched for breakfast when Zander came up behind and put his arms around her.

'You like?'

'I love.' Her head resting against his shoulder, she added dreamily, 'I'm sure it could never look more beautiful than it does at this moment.'

'Before you pass judgement, wait until you've seen it in the fall.'

Thrilled by his words—the continuing relationship they implied—she twisted her head a little to smile up at him.

He bent to kiss the side of her neck, adding to her delight before saying, 'Breakfast's ready when you can bear to tear yourself away.'

Suddenly feeling ravenously hungry, she said, 'I guess that's right now.'

Sitting by the stove, they ate a substantial breakfast of bacon, eggs, mushrooms and hashbrowns while he told her about the lake's wildlife and all that went on locally.

Over coffee they got down to making serious plans for the day. 'Do you ride?' he enquired.

A little surprised, she asked, 'You mean horses?'

'Yes.'

'I used to when I was in my early teens, but I haven't been on a horse since I left school. Why do you ask? Surely there aren't any horses around here?'

'As a matter of fact, Ben keeps a couple of mares which, if you fancy a ride, he'll be happy to lend us. Alternatively, we could drive to Rosedale or go to see Fort Ticonda, or take another trip on the lake, or even...'

He finished detailing the options. Invited to decide, Caris said eagerly, 'You mentioned that somewhere on the far side of the lake there were beavers building a dam—would it be possible to go over and see them?'

'I can't guarantee that we'll see them, but we can certainly try. That is, if you can make it to the Ticonda River on foot. I'm afraid it's impossible to take the boat up, but if we moor at Drystone Creek it's less than a quarter of a mile, and there's a reasonable track. Want to give it a go?'

'Oh, yes please.'

'Then it might be a good idea to take a picnic and make it a full-day trip.'

'Can I help pack the food?'

'Rather than waste time at this end, it might be a good idea to call in at the Lake Store. They pack a quick picnic basket to order, and the store itself is well worth a visit.'

'Sounds great,' she said eagerly.

In a little over five minutes she had been helped aboard

The Swift and they were on their way over the clear, sunlit waters of the lake.

When they reached the Lake Store, she saw it was a long, low, wooden building supported by huge timber piles. There was fancy decking on the three sides that were over the water, and along the frontage were slatted wooden benches interspersed with tubs of bright flowers.

Several boats were already moored, and a kiosk selling ice-cream, newspapers and sundry other items was doing a brisk trade.

To one side, a stand displaying motor oil and various other accessories was flanked by a couple of elderly petrol pumps.

As soon as Zander had tied up and handed her out, he asked for a picnic basket for two then set to work to fill *The Swift*'s tank with fuel while Caris went inside to look around.

With its bare floorboards and open-to-the-rafters ceiling, its series of 'departments' that ran higgledy piggledy into one another—all with mahogany counters and big old-fashioned tills—Lake Store belonged to a bygone age.

It boasted a chandler, a general store with a hardware section, a butcher, a baker and a food area where large bins full of flour, oats, dried fruit, pulses and cereals were fitted with metal scoops and plastic lids.

At the far end was a small diner with an ancient coffee-machine and a soda bar complete with high stools and a jukebox.

The smell of newly baked bread mingled with that of ham and roast beef, oil and paraffin, apples and summer fruits.

Wandering through the general store with its wide variety of household and personal goods, Caris found it as fascinating as Aladdin's cave. There were jeans and tee shirts, socks and sneakers, and a selection of underwear that looked as if it had been there since the year dot.

When Zander appeared to say the picnic basket was packed

and in the boat, she was looking at some large and far from glamorous cotton knickers.

'Oh boy!' He leered at her. 'Were you thinking of buying any of those?'

Trying not to laugh, she said sedately, 'No, I wasn't, as a matter of fact.'

'Perhaps that's just as well. Garments like that could drive a man mad with lust.'

As though overcome by said emotion, he began to growl deep in his throat and bent to bite the side of her neck.

With a little choke of laughter she fled outside as fast as her injured ankle would allow, while Zander paused to speak to someone he knew.

Still smiling, she was sitting on a bench, made into a shady arbour by an arched trellis of rambling roses the colour of buttermilk, when he joined her.

'So, now you've seen our Lake Store, what do you think of it?' he asked quizzically.

'It gave me the impression of being caught in a time warp.'

'So it is.'

'I can't imagine how they're able to provide so many different commodities, and how they manage to find enough staff to run the place.'

'Well, it's a family concern, and as well as Ben and his wife there are seven grown-up children and a couple of grandparents.'

'But where do they all live?'

'Most of them have houses on the lake-shore. A lot of people expected that when the younger generation grew up they'd move nearer to the towns and the bright lights. But there's something about this place that casts a spell...'

'Yes, I know,' Caris agreed wistfully. 'When tomorrow comes, I'll be sorry to leave.'

Watching her face, he remarked thoughtfully, 'We don't

have to leave tomorrow—at least, not unless you want to get home for any reason.'

Choked by a sudden excitement that made her voice husky, she said, 'No, I don't, but...'

'In that case, why not stay?'

'But what about your work?'

'Up to now I haven't taken any time off this year, so I would be more than happy to put everything on hold and have a week's vacation. What do you say?'

'I'd love to,' she agreed with shining eyes.

'Good.' He spoke casually, but his expression told her just how pleased he was.

He was about to rise and help her into the boat when an elderly woman walked past them carrying a large cone of multicoloured ice-cream.

With a grin, Zander asked, 'Fancy an ice-cream before we start?'

She laughed. 'Why not?'

'Any particular flavour?'

Fairly conservative as far as ice-cream went, she answered, 'Vanilla or strawberry, please.'

With a teasing grin, he suggested, 'Why not live dangerously and have both?'

'Why not?'

She waited, drinking in the scent of the roses and caught up in a rainbow bubble of happiness, until he returned with two overflowing cones and sat down by her side.

The reserved, rather shy young woman and the cool, self-contained, sophisticated man were gone. In their places were two carefree people who laughed and talked while they licked their ice-creams like a couple of children.

When they had finished, Zander gave her the little secret smile that she was starting to think of as hers alone; leaning forward, he licked a fleck of ice-cream from the corner of her mouth before kissing her lightly.

His lips were cold—his kiss anything but.

When it finally ended he put an arm round her, drawing her closer. His mouth muffled against her silky hair, he asked softly, 'Have you ever made love in the open air?'

She shook her head.

'Then imagine you and I lying naked together on warm grass, with the sunshine on our skin, a balmy breeze stirring the leaves overhead and only the call of the loons to disturb the silence…'

Her imagination starting to run riot, she shivered.

'Does the thought appeal to you?'

'Well…'

'You don't seem particularly eager. Can it be that I've worn you out?'

'No, it's not that.' Drawing back a little, she said in a rush, 'I'd be afraid of anyone seeing us.'

'I thought you'd decided to live dangerously?'

'Not *that* dangerously.'

He laughed at her heartfelt answer. 'Don't worry, I know a hidden place just off the track we'll be taking, where only the birds will see us.'

'Hmm… Well, perhaps you'd better show me.'

'I was going to say my pleasure, but I'll make sure that it's your pleasure too.'

Her mouth going dry with excitement and anticipation, she allowed herself to be escorted back to the boat and helped in.

When they reached Drystone Creek, Zander moored the boat and handed her out. There wasn't a soul in sight as he picked up a folded blanket and the picnic basket and escorted her up a slight incline to where the trees started.

'Go carefully,' he warned. 'We don't want any further damage to that ankle.'

About a hundred yards along the track, he turned and led the way past a large notice nailed to a tree that read: PRIVATE PROPERTY. KEEP OUT.

Sensing her reluctance to venture any further, he said, 'Don't worry. This land belongs to Ben, and I have his full permission to be on it.'

A moment later they were making their way through what had at first appeared to be an impenetrable thicket. For a few yards the going was difficult, then they emerged into a clear area with a shallow sunlit knoll which Zander helped her climb, an arm around her waist.

She was wondering how the top of a rounded hill could truly be described as 'hidden' when she saw there was a grassy hollow in the centre, partially shaded by a single tree.

It was a most delightful spot.

Having put the picnic basket in the shade, Zander spread the blanket on the sun-dappled grass and, taking her hands, drew her into the hollow and laid her down.

As he stretched out by her side and began to kiss her, a thought struck her that made her tense.

Lifting his head, he enquired, 'Something wrong?'

Finding the notion quite intolerable, she blurted out, 'How did you know this was the perfect spot for love-making?'

He frowned. 'You mean have I ever brought another woman here?'

Looking up into his face, she demanded raggedly, 'Well, have you?'

'No, I haven't.'

There was an unmistakable ring of truth in his voice that convinced her.

'The last time I was up at Square Lake,' he went on evenly, 'I happened to be walking this way and I stopped where we are now to eat my lunch. It seemed to be an idyllic spot, and the thought crossed my mind that if I ever found a woman as perfect I'd bring her here.'

'I'm sorry.' Filled with gladness, she threw her arms around his neck and, drawing him down to her, she kissed him.

'Hmm…' he murmured, his lips brushing hers. 'A response like this is worth a moment of doubt.'

Between kisses sweeter than wine, he whispered how lovely she was, how much she entranced him, how wonderful it was to make love to someone who was like an eager flame in his arms.

Unbearably moved, she said a shade mockingly, 'How very romantic.'

Playfully, he nipped her ear lobe between his teeth. 'So you prefer a more down-to-earth approach? In that event, get yer kit off and give us a kiss.'

She gave a little choke of laughter. 'Fool!'

He sighed melodramatically. 'Some women don't know what they do want. How about handcuffs and a whip?'

'No thanks,' she declined hastily. 'If it's all the same to you, I'll stick with something a shade less, shall we say, exciting.'

'Such as good, honest, joyful sex?'

'Suits me fine. And I've really no objection to a spot of romance. In fact, I rather like it,' she added demurely, fluttering her eyelashes at him.

It was his turn to laugh. 'Then never fear, I'm sure I can oblige…'

CHAPTER SEVEN

THAT afternoon, after eating an excellent lunch and spending a fascinating hour watching the beavers building their dam, they set off back down the track.

Their decision to stay for the week made it necessary to go to Hallgarth to fetch Caris's things. That being the case, when they had returned the picnic basket, they went straight back to Owl Lodge instead of carrying on with their planned trip to see the Lion Rock.

The car keys in his hand, Zander asked, 'Do you want to come with me, or would you rather stay here?'

'I'll come with you,' she answered without hesitation, and earned herself a kiss.

The journey was a pleasant one, but by the time they reached Hallgarth it had turned seven-thirty and they were both hungry.

'As far as I can see we have two options,' Zander remarked. 'We can either have a leisurely meal here and stay the night, or we can start back at once and stop for a meal on the way. Which do you prefer?'

Unsure which he would prefer, she thought for a moment. He didn't look tired so, taking a gamble, she admitted, 'I'd sooner start back at once.'

She knew by his face that she had made the right decision, even before he said, 'That's exactly what I wanted to hear. I'll just put your things in the car and we'll get straight off. We can stop for dinner in Daintree; it's only about half an hour's journey and a relatively short detour from our normal route.'

After a very good meal at Daintree's White Bear, it was quite late when they got back to Owl Lodge. While Zander threw logs on the stove and locked up for the night, Caris went straight to bed.

She had intended to stay awake until he joined her, but she slept the instant her head touched the pillow, and when he got in beside her and gathered her close she just sighed in her sleep and nestled against him.

The days that followed were exciting and blissful—the nights even more so—and, as the hot weather they both loved turned into a heatwave with soaring temperatures, they made the most of it.

They ate al fresco, went on trips by car and boat, took morning swims in the lake, rode Ben's horses and, the moment her ankle would allow, walked for miles.

Sometimes they talked, sometimes they remained silent, but always the warmth and closeness, the harmony of companionship, was there.

Each morning, sitting on the swing seat on the front porch, they drank their coffee and made plans for the day while the lake stirred into life.

Each evening, entwined in each other's arms, they sipped wine as they watched the play of moonbeams across the water before going to bed.

Caris had more than once imagined how wonderful and romantic it would be, but she was forced to admit that the reality was even better.

The heatwave brought along with it a warm summer wind and, taking full advantage, they went sailing on *The Loon* for an hour or so almost every day.

When Caris took to sailing like a duck took to water,

Zander was delighted and started to teach her how to handle the boat.

As the days slipped past she learnt a lot about him, about what kind of man he was, and liked what she learnt.

Though he was anything but soft—in fact in some ways he could be quite formidable—he was kind and compassionate, with a strong sense of justice and fair play.

Good-tempered and well-balanced, he had a spiky sense of humour, an endless patience and a zest for life that was invigorating.

All in all he was exactly the kind of man she had been waiting for, and each day she fell a little more in love with him.

She recognized with a quiet happiness that what she felt for Zander was nothing at all like what she had felt for Karl.

The passion and sexual chemistry was incredible, and mingled with those emotions was a steady warmth, a genuine affection, a *liking*, which she now realized was as necessary as the loving.

She was made even happier by the growing certainty that Zander felt the same way about her, and she gave thanks for those sunny days together. Days that she never wanted to end.

But Sunday brought the realization that their idyll was almost over; early the next morning she would have to go back to Albany and her everyday life.

Unwilling to blight their last day, however, she tried to push the thought to the back of her mind.

After a lovely day spent in Ticonda, they decided to take one of the town's specialities back with them and eat on their own porch, instead of having dinner in a crowded restaurant.

As they waited in the open air for the spit-roasted chicken to finishing cooking, a stray cloud drifted over and some heavy spots of warm summer rain started to fall.

Zander handed Caris the key to the car which was parked

close by and suggested, 'Why don't you put the roof up and wait in the car?'

Reluctant to leave his side even for a moment, she hesitated briefly before obeying.

When he joined her a few minutes later carrying a neatly boxed chicken under his arm, his shirt was damp and his fair hair darkened by the rain.

Sliding in beside her, he gave her a smile and, leaning over, kissed her as though he had disliked that briefest of partings as much as she had.

The rain was short-lived, and by the time they got back to Square Lake the air was clear and golden, the evening perfect for eating on the porch.

It wasn't until the meal was over and they were sitting looking at the lovely view that Zander broached the subject of going back.

His arm tightening round her, he said, 'Though there's nothing I'd like better than to stay here indefinitely, tomorrow we shall have to return to the real world...'

Listening to the strange, eerie cry of the loons echoing across the water, and watching the black shapes of bats flitting about in the balmy twilight, she agreed with a sigh, 'Yes, I know.'

He seemed about to say something else, something of importance, but when he did speak it was only to ask, 'Ready for bed?'

When she nodded, he rose to his feet with her in his arms. But instead of going straight inside he paused for them to take one last look at the serene, shining lake and the blue mountains with skeins of silver-edged, purple cloud gathering on their peaks.

Overnight the heatwave broke, and by dawn the mountains were obscured by fine veils of rain that drifted over the lake and shrouded the trees.

Waking to the realization that their time here was over, Caris felt a wrenching sense of loss that something beautiful, something that could never be recaptured, was coming to an end.

Watching her transparent face, Zander drew her close and kissed her, before making love to her with an urgency that seemed to echo that feeling.

Afterwards they showered and ate an early breakfast by the fire, then Zander packed the car, and all too quickly they were drawing away from Owl Lodge and leaving paradise behind them.

'Sorry to leave?' he asked as they crossed the shallow creek.

Too choked to speak, she nodded.

One hand left the steering wheel to give her a comforting squeeze. 'We'll be back.'

Though she desperately wanted to believe it, a kind of premonition made her unable to.

As she surreptitiously felt in her bag for a tissue, he asked, 'Do you want me to take you back to your own flat?'

She blew her nose. 'Where else could I go?'

He said what he had been afraid to say the previous night. 'You could move in with me…'

Taken completely by surprise, she gaped at him.

'Unless your father would disapprove?'

'I'm nearly twenty-four and my own mistress,' she pointed out. 'In any case, as long as I do my work, my father has no interest in my private life.'

'Then, to borrow a phrase from Marlowe, "Come live with me and be my love…"'

Her heart swelling at his words, and swamped by a blinding wave of love, Caris leaned her head against his shoulder.

'Is that a yes?' he asked. Feeling her nod, he turned so that his lips touched her hair. 'That's good.' He added a shade

huskily, 'I really don't know what I would have done if you'd
said no.'

Floating on cloud nine, she made an effort to bring her
feet back to earth, by asking, 'How long does it take to drive
from Hallgarth to Albany?'

'I wasn't thinking of living at Hallgarth during the week,
it's a bit too far to commute comfortably. That's why I decided to buy the apartment for when I'm working in Albany.
I dislike staying in hotels.'

'Too much like a busman's holiday?'

'Exactly. But the apartment's quite small, really just a pied-
à-terre, so we'll need to start looking for something bigger.'

But as far as Caris was concerned, wherever he was would
be akin to paradise.

One unexpected stumbling block, however, had been her
father's reaction. She had presumed he wouldn't care what
she did but, having learnt her intention, he'd demanded, 'Who
the devil is this man? You can't have known him very long?'

When she'd admitted she hadn't, he'd gone through the
roof. 'Have you gone absolutely mad! After the way you've
worked, how can you risk jeopardizing your entire career for
someone you don't really know?'

'It won't make any difference to my career,' she pleaded.
'I intend to keep on working.'

'You're talking like a fool!' he stormed. 'You can't possibly
give your mind to your work when some man is taking over
your life. I thought you'd have more sense than to let sex—'

'It isn't just sex,' she broke in determinedly. 'We love each
other.'

Yet even as the words passed her lips she wondered, did
Zander really love her? He'd said he wanted her, said she was
special, but he had never actually said he loved her...

But her father was going on. 'Apparently he doesn't love

you enough to want to marry you, so why throw everything away you've already achieved?'

Seeing the stubborn set of her chin, he added furiously, 'You'll never be given a partnership if you don't get rid of him and concentrate one-hundred percent on your work…'

But for once in her life Caris chose to defy her father. Eager as a young Juliet, she left the furnished apartment she shared with Mitch and moved her relatively few personal belongings into Zander's.

At his suggestion, she gave her old car to her ex-flatmate and started to use one of his.

For a while, in spite of her father's bitter and continued opposition, she was deliriously happy. Then, right out of the blue, things started to go badly wrong…

A loud crack of thunder and a fresh flurry of rain lashing Gracedieu's leaded windows.

Caris looked up with something of a shock to find that Zander was watching her intently.

Beyond the range of the fire-glow the room seemed dark and chill, but within the semi-circle of warmth and light it was comfortable—cosy, even.

But in spite of the ease and intimacy suggested by the proximity of the two chairs the atmosphere was still taut, and she jumped when Zander remarked, 'You've been miles away. Reliving the past?'

'No,' she lied. 'I try not to think about the past. It's over and done with. Dead.'

'Now there we disagree. The past is never really dead. It makes us what we are today.'

As he spoke, blue-white lightning flashed, illuminating the room, while wind beat against the windows and howled in the chimney like a banshee.

Desperate to change the subject, she said quickly, 'I'm really sorry about the weather.'

'Though you have a lot to answer for, I can hardly blame you for the weather.'

Pierced to the heart, she asked hoarsely, 'What do you mean, "a lot to answer for"?'

'I mean the way you ran out on me.'

She felt a quick surge of relief that it wasn't the accusation she'd been most afraid of.

'How do you think I felt when I got home that night and discovered you'd packed your things and left without a word?'

Though he spoke quietly, it was obvious that he was struggling with some powerful emotion.

The breath caught in her throat. She realized that she had been quite wrong when she had thought him indifferent. His feelings were clearly very strong, but whether it was anger or hatred he felt she wasn't sure. Both, perhaps.

Suddenly it was all too much. More than she felt she could bear.

But she had to bear it. She had no choice. Somehow, having got into this predicament, she had to carry it through with as much composure as she could muster.

Taking a deep breath and doing her utmost to sound cool and businesslike, she said crisply, 'I really can't stay here any longer. I ought to be showing you the estate. After all, that's what I'm here for.'

When he merely looked at her, she went on, 'I admit that the conditions aren't good, but if we just drive round it'll give you some idea.'

Making no comment, he stayed where he was, lounging back in his chair, appearing at ease, totally relaxed, master of the situation.

But on closer observation she noticed a latent tension she'd missed at first glance. Her eyes moved to his handsome face and she saw he looked drawn, tired to death.

Rising to her feet, she urged jerkily, 'Shall we get on? The storm seems to be easing off a little.'

Another bright flash of lightning and a further onslaught of rain against the windowpanes gave the lie to her words.

'That sounds remarkably like wishful thinking,' he observed ironically.

'I suppose it does,' she was forced to admit. 'It's just that I should be working.'

'Think of this as working.'

She looked at him.

'Isn't keeping a prospective buyer happy an essential part of your job?'

'Well, yes,' she admitted.

'And, in view of the amount of money involved, I imagine I rate as a fairly important buyer?'

There was no need to answer.

'That being the case, presumably you came hoping to clinch the deal?'

Knowing it was useless to deny it, she agreed reluctantly, 'You could say that.'

'Well, to have any chance of succeeding,' he told her, raising an eyebrow, 'You'll need to pander to me.'

Registering the expression of mingled dismay and vexation on her face, he went on, 'So for heaven's sake stop hovering. Sit down again and try to relax.'

Seeing nothing else for it, Caris did as she had been bidden.

She was afraid he would bring up the past once more, but he seemed in no hurry to break the silence. While she waited for the storm to subside, she simply sat and gazed into the fire.

The deep pile of glowing embers, the leaping flames, the

bright sparks that flew upwards when one of the logs settled, proved to be almost hypnotic.

Tired after the previous night's disturbed sleep and emotionally drained, she felt her eyelids begin to droop.

Watching her, Zander thought she was even lovelier than he remembered. Then, her beauty had been fresh and untouched, that of a girl. Now it was that of a mature woman, with a sadness, a vulnerability, a poignancy, that was haunting.

Realizing that she was in danger of drifting off, Caris stirred herself and glanced up to find that Zander was watching her through half-closed lids.

The expression of mingled pain and longing on his face made her catch her breath but in an instant a shutter came down, hiding his emotions.

Disturbed afresh, she moved restlessly.

'Something wrong?' he asked.

'I was just wondering how much longer it'll be before we can go.'

'Hard to say. We could be here for hours yet.'

'I certainly hope not!' she exclaimed with feeling. He clicked his tongue reprovingly. 'That's a black mark against you.'

Then, with mockery in his green eyes he went on, 'As a valuable potential buyer, the very least you could do is *pretend* to be enjoying my company.'

Realizing he was out to rattle her, and knowing the only way she could hope to win was by playing him at his own game, she retorted with saccharine sweetness, 'How could you doubt it?'

He raised an eyebrow. 'Then why sound as if you couldn't wait to get away?'

She said the first thing that came into her head. 'It's just that I'm dying for a cup of coffee.'

'That's not a bad idea. I'll see what I can do.'

'If you can rustle up some coffee, I'll give you full marks. But in my opinion you'll need to be a miracle worker.'

'I'm afraid I can't claim to be that. But we do have running water and—' he leaned forward to poke the fire, sending the orange flames leaping '—a good, hot stove to heat it on.'

'So all we lack is the coffee,' she murmured drily.

Undaunted, he said, 'Oh, you never know. There's quite a lot of stuff left in the cupboards. I'll take a look.' He rose to his feet.

On one of her previous visits, whilst glancing in the various cupboards to assess the storage space, Caris had noticed quite a good supply of tinned food and store-cupboard items, but she had seen no sign of any coffee.

She shook her head. 'I rather think you'll be wasting your time.'

'Want to bet?' he asked jokingly.

In the same vein, she answered, 'I was taught never to bet for money.'

'So what shall we bet for? What would you like if you win?'

Fairly confident of doing just that, she took a deep breath and chanced his wrath. 'I'd like to leave here straight away, regardless of the weather.'

'Very well. And if *I* win—' he pretended to consider '—let's say...a kiss for old times' sake, shall we?'

Sudden panic had her blurting out, 'No! No, I—'

'Afraid of losing?' he taunted.

'Not at all. But if there *is* any coffee, it has to be fit to drink.'

'That goes without saying.'

She pressed home her advantage. 'Let's say an unopened pack or jar.'

'Unopened?' He ran thoughtful fingers over his chin before agreeing. 'Okay.'

For no good reason, his prompt acceptance of her terms
made her feel a shade uneasy.

Watching her expressive face, he asked, 'So is the bet on?
Or do you want to chicken out?'

Dismissing the unease and telling herself they would soon
be out of here, she informed him decidedly, 'The bet's on.'

'Good,' Zander said with soft satisfaction and, crossing the
kitchen, he opened the door of one of the huge cupboards.

As she watched incredulously, he reached up to the second
shelf and produced a cafetière and a sealed pack of coffee.

'I'm afraid we'll have to drink it black, but in the circumstances...'

Feeling as if she had been winded, she asked hoarsely,
'How did you know they were there?'

'I noticed them earlier,' he admitted.

As if reading her unspoken thoughts, he added, 'They
were a little way back, so unless you were six inches taller
you wouldn't have noticed them.'

Biting her lip, she silently berated herself for being fool
enough to bet. She should have realized he was setting a trap.

Having half-filled the cafetière with water, he spooned in
the coffee and set it on the stove. Then while it heated, he
pulled the low table into place and found and rinsed a couple
of mugs.

When the cafetière started to bubble and the fragrant aroma
of coffee drifted on the air he filled the mugs and set one in
front of her.

Dropping into the chair opposite, with a glance at the
streaming windows he observed, 'It seems to be raining
harder than ever.'

'Well, we can't stay here much longer,' she burst out.

'Why not? We're warm and comfortable, and the cupboards are well stocked with canned food, so we can rustle up a meal of some kind if we get hungry.'

It sounded very much as if he was pleased by the prospect. Convinced now that he was playing some kind of cat-and-mouse game, keeping her here while he waited for her to crack, her blood ran cold.

But she was determined not to give him the satisfaction of seeing how rattled she was. She bit back the panicky rush of words that rose to her lips and, trying to look unmoved, picked up her mug of coffee.

But he hadn't failed to notice her agitation, and as she prepared to take a sip he warned, 'Careful; it's very hot, and I wouldn't like you to burn your mouth.' With a little mocking smile, he added, 'I haven't yet collected on our bet.'

It sounded like a threat and she had to repress a shiver. She couldn't bear it if he kissed her.

While she made a pretence of drinking her coffee, she tried to focus, to sort out something workable from the seething mass of thoughts filling her head.

Suppose she simply refused to stay any longer? It wasn't professional, and it could well mean losing the sale. But there were other people interested, she reminded herself.

A sudden, disturbing thought brought her up short. What if he wouldn't allow her to leave? What if he was determined to drag up the traumatic past—ask questions she didn't want to answer?

Don't be a fool, she scolded herself, *he can't make you stay.*

But in her heart of hearts she knew he could if he so wished. He was much bigger and stronger than she was, and if he was angry enough to coerce her...

A glance in his direction showed he had finished his own coffee and was leaning back, enjoying the warmth with cat-like indolence, his eyes closed.

Perhaps to make things easy she could slip out while he was dozing? It would mean leaving him to lock up, but surely he would do that? And when he returned the keys to the office she would take care not to be alone.

For a while she watched him surreptitiously, then when he showed no sign of stirring she rose to her feet, picked up her bag and briefcase and, leaving the bunch of keys on the table, moved noiselessly towards the door.

'Going somewhere?' The lazy enquiry stopped her in her tracks.

Her heart throwing itself against her ribs, she turned to look at him. He didn't appear to have moved, but now she could see the gleam of his eyes through their thick curtain of lashes.

'I have to get back to the office.' Relieved that her voice was steady, she added, 'I take it that you'll lock up when you leave?'

'Isn't abandoning a potential buyer rather unprofessional?' he asked mildly.

'It depends on the buyer.'

'Very well, run. But you can't go on running. I know where to find you, and sooner or later you're going to have to talk to me, face up to the past.'

Closing her mind to his words, she fled.

The rain was still torrential, bouncing off the paving stones, gurgling in the gutters, dripping from the climbing plants and streaming down the shallow channel that directed it away from the house.

Though her car was quite close, without a mac she was saturated in seconds. Pulling open the door, struggling to hold it against the wind, she jumped in. Too relieved that she had escaped to worry about her drenched state, she wiped water from her eyes, fastened her seat belt and turned the key in the ignition.

There was a click, then nothing.

Taking a deep breath, she tried again.

Still nothing.

The problem she'd had starting the car earlier had gone clean out of her head, and now she groaned.

Why did it have to happen today of all days?

Driven by desperation, it took several more tries to convince her that it wasn't going to fire; the engine was dead.

Which meant she would have to wait for a taxi.

While the lightning flashed and thunder ripped the heavens apart, she opened her bag and felt for her phone.

When she couldn't immediately find it, she looked more carefully.

Still it failed to come to light.

It took a third and more thorough search to convince her it wasn't there.

Her heart like lead, she realized she mustn't have picked it up that morning. Harassed by her dream and thoughts of the past, hurrying to try and leave them behind, she must have left it on charge.

Now what was she to do? Though Zander's hired car was standing there, she couldn't—wouldn't—ask him for help.

But what if he'd left the car unlocked and the keys in the ignition?

Choked by excitement, she pulled on her mac, struggled out and hurried towards his car buffeted by the wind and rain.

The door was unlocked, but to her disappointment the ignition was empty.

Unless she was willing to return with her tail between her legs—which she wasn't—that left her with just one option: to walk as far as the road and try to get a lift back to town.

With the storm still raging it wasn't a pleasant prospect, but she was already cold and soaked to the skin so it wouldn't make all that much difference, she told herself stoutly.

As she turned, a fierce gust of wind sent her staggering off balance; she stumbled and fell, grazing her shins and knees on the rough stone.

Picking herself up, she gritted her teeth and, head down against the elements, started for the driveway.

She had only gone a matter of yards when her arm was caught and held. His voice raised above the noise of the storm, Zander was demanding, 'What on earth do you think you're doing? Where are you going?'

Pulling her arm free, she told him shortly, 'My car won't start and I've forgotten my phone, so I'm going to try and get a lift back to town.'

Holding on to his patience, he pointed out, 'The drive must be the best part of a mile long, and even if you get as far as the road there aren't likely to be many cars out and about in these conditions.'

As he spoke an extra-strong gust sent them both staggering.

'Don't be a fool,' he urged. 'You'll never make it. Come back inside.'

The rain was beating into her face and the wind was stopping her breath. She hesitated. Then, feeling suddenly exhausted, chilled to the bone and trembling in every limb, she allowed herself be hurried into the house and back to the warmth of the kitchen.

Dripping wet and still shaking, she went to stand by the stove. She looked a sorry sight. Stray wisps of hair hung around her pale face, blood trickled down her legs and a puddle of water was starting to form at her feet.

Zander was equally wet, his fair hair plastered to his head, rain drops running down his face, his clothes clinging to his tall frame.

She rounded on him and, through teeth that had started to chatter, cried, 'Damn you! This is all your fault.'

Wiping water out of his eyes, he said mildly, 'Do I take it you're blaming me for the inclement weather, for your car refusing to start and for the absence of your cell phone?'

Suddenly ashamed of her outburst, she said, 'No, of course not. I'm sorry.' Then before he could crow any more she went on, 'But you *are* to blame for insisting on staying here.'

'May I point out that if you *had* stayed here neither of us would be in the state we're in? But, rather than stand arguing, I suggest we get ourselves dried.'

'What on?' she asked raggedly. 'A sheepskin rug?'

'I think a towel might be a better bet.' He opened one of the linen cupboards and took out a big white towel. 'You can even have a different colour, if you prefer.'

'Full marks,' she muttered, savagely sarcastic. 'You seem able to produce everything that's needed.'

'Not quite everything. A change of clothes, though perhaps not essential as we know each other so well, would have been handy.'

Watching her bite her lip, he added, 'But in the circumstances we'll have to manage with a bathrobe. And I'm afraid that this time you don't have a choice. It's navy-blue or nothing.'

'My favourite colour!'

He raised an eyebrow. Handing her a folded robe, he suggested, 'If you want to strip off by the stove where it's warmer, I'll use the bathroom. Unless you'd like me to stay here with you?'

'No, I wouldn't!'

Grinning at her vehemence, he took a towel, one of the robes and departed.

As soon as the door had closed behind him, Caris removed her sodden shoes and her ruined tights, peeled off her wet clothes and dried herself thoroughly before donning the towelling robe and belting it securely.

It was a man's robe and much too big for her, but it was blessedly warm, and once she had turned up the sleeves it was comfortable to wear.

Having searched in her handbag for a comb, she removed the pins from what remained of her knot, towelled her long hair, combed out the tangles and left it loose around her shoulders to finish drying.

Then all at once reaction set in. Her legs feeling scarcely able to support her, she abandoned her saturated belongings by the hearth and, with a weird feeling that she was reliving a scene that had taken place almost three years ago at Owl Lodge, resumed her seat close to the fire.

CHAPTER EIGHT

She had barely sat down when Zander reappeared wearing a matching robe and queried solicitously, 'Feeling warmer now?'

Holding back her anger and frustration, she answered stiffly, 'Yes, thank you.'

'Good.' He was carrying his own wet things and when he had gathered hers up too he headed for the deep porcelain sink.

After removing as much water as possible from the garments, he hung them on a slatted airer suspended from the ceiling, commenting, 'The air's quite warm now, so with a bit of luck they should soon start to dry. Though it's going to take some time,' he added as he pulled the wooden contraption up and secured the cord.

Caris gritted her teeth. Events seemed to be repeating themselves. It was as though she had been caught in some kind of time-warp and travelled back three years.

When she remained silent, he glanced at her; noticing the blood still oozing from the grazes, he remarked, 'Your legs are still bleeding; I'd better take a look.'

'There's no need,' she said sharply. 'It's only a few scrapes.'

'They may need cleaning; earlier I noticed some antiseptic pads and cream in one of the drawers.'

Having located both items, he came to stand in front of her. 'Let me see.'

Knowing only too well that he wasn't about to take no for an answer, she held the robe closely around her thighs and reluctantly stretched out her legs.

Zander squatted down in front of her and began to wipe away the blood and gently clean the grazes on her knees and shins.

She stared down at his well-shaped head, his damp, slightly rumpled hair and neatly set ears. With a tug at her heartstrings, she recalled a previous occasion when he had crouched at her feet and played the role of nurse.

She also recalled, with a sudden flare of alarm, the unprecedented effect it had had on her.

But even as she told herself that things were very different this time—that she wouldn't let his nearness, the touch of his hands, move her in the slightest—she felt that old familiar warmth rising inside her.

He glanced up and smiled a little, as though he knew exactly what she was thinking and feeling.

Her face growing hot, she looked hastily away.

When he had finished applying a light film of antiseptic cream, he remarked, 'There, that should help to ease the soreness.'

'Thank you,' she said in a constrained voice.

Having used a pad to remove the grease from his fingers, he put everything neatly back in the drawer before starting to make some fresh coffee.

When it was made and poured, he passed her a mug. Resuming his seat, he leaned back, his bare feet extended towards the blaze.

To an onlooker the little scene would have appeared tranquil, companionable, but in reality anger and resentment laced the air and tension stretched between them, dangerous as barbed wire.

When both their mugs were empty, he enquired solicitously, 'More coffee?'

She shook her head.

'Anything you would like?'

'Yes. I'd like to know how long you're intending to stay here.'

'Well, we can't really go until our clothes are dry.'

'Please don't play games with me,' she said sharply. 'How long?'

'For as long as it takes.'

'To do what?'

'To break down the barriers you've erected and get through to you. I need you to talk to me, to tell me exactly why you left me.'

But she couldn't bear to talk about the past, to have all her pain, misery and guilt dragged into the open.

'I've no intention of talking about the past. You're only wasting your time.'

He shrugged. 'I've plenty of it.'

Thoroughly rattled now, she burst out, 'Well, I haven't. If I'm not home by this evening, people will miss me.'

'Oh? Which people in particular?'

After a moment of complete blankness, she stammered, 'M-my aunt, for one.'

Zander shook his head. 'I think not. I happen to know that your aunt died about two years ago.'

Watching her jaw drop, he added, 'Oh yes, since finding you I've done my homework.

'I'm sorry about your aunt. She couldn't have been very old; what did she die of?'

Losing her beloved aunt had been a big blow, and Caris's

voice was unsteady as she told him, 'She had what should have been just a minor operation, and died of septicaemia.'

'That must have been tough.'

Brushing aside what she saw as spurious sympathy, she demanded, 'How long have you known where I was?'

'I only found out quite recently.'

'How?'

'By chance. I was in England when I happened to read an article about Gracedieu being on the market. Your name was mentioned as the sole agent, and there was a photograph of you. I asked Michael Grayson's PA to make an appointment.'

So she had been completely mistaken in believing that meeting Zander again was just a devastating coincidence.

Though she was already sure of the answer, she asked, 'Why did you use Michael Grayson's name?'

He answered her question with a question of his own. 'Would you have shown up if you'd known in advance who the buyer was?'

After a swift glance at her face, he said grimly, 'No, I didn't think so.'

He stopped speaking and the silence lengthened—a silence that was far from companionable. Though they were together physically, mentally they were miles apart, a no-man's-land of unspoken questions and answers, of shattered expectations and dashed hopes stretching between them.

In complete contrast she found herself recalling the past, how close they had once been, how they had sat by the stove at Owl Lodge, together in every sense of the word, and all at once her deep-blue eyes filled with tears.

Hoping against hope that he wouldn't look up, she tried not to blink. But despite all her efforts the tears escaped and rolled slowly down her cheeks in tracks of shiny wetness.

Afraid to wipe them away in case he noticed, she stayed as still as a statue.

Perhaps it was that very stillness that alerted him, because he suddenly glanced up. Rising to his feet in a single, swift movement, he came to stand by her side.

As she sat mute and mortified, he caught a single bright teardrop with his index finger.

She flinched away as though he had struck her.

'Why the tears?'

'I was thinking about the Gracedieu estate,' she lied desperately.

'Really?'

Though it was obvious he didn't believe a word of it, she found herself babbling, 'I was disappointed that you never had any intention of buying it.'

Resuming his seat, Zander drawled, 'My, but you do take your job seriously.'

Feeling a little easier now he wasn't looming over her, she shook her head. 'In this case it's not just a job. I fell in love with the place at first sight, and I hate the thought of possibly having to sell it off piecemeal.'

'There, now! That just shows how wrong one can be. You were worrying about Gracedieu, when I could have sworn you were thinking about the past.'

'I try not to think about the past.' Without intending to, she found herself adding bitterly, 'It hurts too much.'

His eyes darkened to a deep, cloudy jade. 'No matter how much it hurts, the past has to be faced sooner or later.'

Seeing her white, set face, the misery in her eyes, he decided it would be better to skirt the main issue for the moment. He said more gently, 'Why not tell me what happened after our quarrel?'

So long as she left out the one thing she couldn't bear to talk about, she could tell him the rest, Caris thought.

Taking a deep, steadying breath, she began, 'When you'd left for the office I packed my things.'

'Yes,' he said bleakly. 'It wasn't until I discovered they'd gone that I truly believed you'd leave me without a word. Where did you go?'

'At first I didn't know where to go or what to do...' Her voice shook and she stopped speaking as she recalled the feeling of utter desolation that had gripped her.

As soon as she could trust herself to go on, she continued. 'There was no way I could keep on working for my father. His anger and disapproval, his "I told you so" attitude, would have made my life a misery—so I urgently needed to find another job and somewhere to live.

'I decided to get right away from Albany.' Her worst fear had been that she might run into Zander if she stayed. 'In the end, I made up my mind to go back to England, to Aunt Jo. I hired a car to drive to JFK, and as soon as I got there I booked a seat on the first available plane to London.

'While I was waiting for the flight to be called, I rang Aunt Jo to tell her I was on my way. She came to the airport and met me with open arms.'

Remembering just how much her aunt's warm welcome had meant to her that dreadful day, Caris had to stop and wipe away the tears.

'Then you were living in Spitewinter right from the word go?'

'Yes.'

He sighed. 'I ought to have had more sense than believe her.'

Caris was about to ask him what he meant when he went on, 'That night when I got back and found you'd gone, I was devastated. After I'd tried all the local hotels without success I went to see your father. I didn't expect you to be with him, but I thought he might know where you were.

'Even before he knew the reason for my visit he was somewhat less than cordial, and when he *did* know he really let rip. He said that in his opinion you'd been a complete fool to take up with me in the first place, and it was a great pity you'd come to your senses too late. He added with some venom that it had probably ruined both your life and your career prospects.

'When I refused to get into a verbal fight, and simply emphasized that I needed to find you without delay, he told me scathingly that I'd get no help from him. He didn't know where you'd gone, and if he had known he wouldn't have told me. That said, he practically ordered me out.

'Then it occurred to me rather belatedly that you might have gone back to the apartment you'd once shared with Miss Mitchell. But when I went round I could get no answer, and the next-door neighbour told me that the young lady who lived there was still away on a course of some kind.

'I was racking my brains over what to do next when I remembered you mentioning living with an Aunt Jo while you were at university in England. I didn't know her surname, however, and all I could recall was that she lived in a vicarage somewhere on the borders of Cambridgeshire.

'I decided to approach your uncle, but when I called in at the Belmont offices he refused point-blank to see me or give me any information, and ordered his secretary to show me out.

'In desperation I tried your old apartment again, and this time Miss Mitchell was home. She said she hadn't seen you and had no idea where you were. But she *was* able to tell me your aunt's surname and where she lived. I got on the next plane to England in high hopes that you might be with her, or that she would be able to tell me your whereabouts.

'However, when I arrived on her doorstep she swore she hadn't seen you since you finished university and went back to the States.'

Knocked sideways by what he was telling her, Caris protested weakly, 'It wasn't like Aunt Jo to lie. Usually she was the most truthful of people and kindness itself.'

'Oh, she was kind, all right,' Zander agreed wryly. 'She said what a shame it was that I'd had a wasted journey, and promised to let me know if she heard from you. She added that, if it was any help, you'd always wanted to live in New York City and she thought it more than likely that you'd gone there. But I presume you already knew most of that,' he ended bleakly.

Feeling as if she had been stabbed to the heart, Caris shook her head. 'I had no idea you'd been over. She never said a word to me.'

She went on unsteadily, 'But I believe I know why she didn't tell me. She must have been trying to protect me from any more unhappiness.'

With a kind of urgency, Zander asked, 'Would it have made any difference if she *had* told you?'

The question tightened round her throat like a silken noose. *Would* it have made any difference if she had known Zander was actively looking for her?

She tried to tell herself it wouldn't have. But she couldn't be sure…

Don't be an idiot, she silently adjured herself. She couldn't have *let* it make any difference. Nothing could alter the fact that he had never intended their relationship to be permanent, had never really loved her. Shaking her head, she answered sadly, 'No, it wouldn't have made any difference.'

His voice cold as winter, he said, 'I guess I was a fool to expect anything else.' He went on heavily, 'But at that time I still had hopes that I could find you and put everything right, so I hired a firm of detectives to keep looking. Because of what your aunt had said, they focused on New York. But New York is a big place with millions of people, and it was like trying to find a needle in a haystack.

'They were still looking when I saw the article about Gracedieu being for sale and knew the search was finally over...'

So he had been trying to find her for three years? 'After the appointment to view the place had been safely made, I tried to possess my soul in patience while I waited to see you, but the days in between seemed endless.'

Her thoughts were all over the place; she asked, 'If you wanted to see me so badly, why didn't you simply come into the agency?'

'Because we had a lot of things to talk about and I wanted time and privacy, somewhere we could be quite alone, where we wouldn't be interrupted. That's why meeting you here seemed ideal.'

Filled with trepidation, she asked, 'But why go to so much trouble to try to dig up the past? Surely you had nothing to gain after all this time?'

'That's just where you're wrong. I have a great deal to gain.'

'Such as?'

'Some answers to my questions and, hopefully, peace of mind.'

Scared of where this was going, she stayed silent.

'You'll never know how many sleepless nights you caused me. Nights when I lay awake wondering where you were and worrying about what was happening to you. Nights when I longed to hold you in my arms again and make love to you...'

There was so much passion in his voice, so much pain, that Caris felt as if she were drowning in it.

But why were his feelings so intense now? After those first happy months together, he had seemed to change completely, and during the final few weeks of their relationship it had been only too clear that he'd no longer cared—if he ever had.

When Karl had tired of her she had emerged from the affair relatively unscathed, apart from hurt pride and an abiding sense of shame. Her heart and her deepest feelings had been untouched.

But with Zander she had given her heart and everything else she had to give, and the consequences had been catastrophic.

Watching her catch her underlip in her teeth, and realizing that she might be wavering at last, he urged, 'Tell me why you ran as you did. Talk to me, Caris—make me understand.'

He had said it was time she stopped running and faced the past, and maybe it was.

She had thought of their relationship—an enchanted, whirlwind love-affair—as untouchable, inviolate, built on a foundation of caring so strong that it would last a lifetime.

It had been almost impossible to believe that anything could go wrong. Then real life had taken over and the whole magical edifice had collapsed, crumbled into dust, leaving her abandoned in the ruins of her cherished hopes and dreams.

She had closed in on herself, bottled things up, endeavoured to shut out the past. But in spite of all her efforts it hadn't really worked.

Perhaps if she talked to Zander—voiced all her pain and disillusionment, looked the past in the face—it would allow her to come to terms with the failure of their relationship, so that the failure no longer had the power to hurt.

It was worth a try.

Though there was one thing she might never come to terms with. One thing that would always hurt to some extent. One thing she was desperate to keep from him at all costs.

Pushing that thing to the back of her mind, she drew a deep breath and took the plunge. 'I went because I couldn't bear to stay with a man I knew no longer wanted me.'

He looked taken aback. 'You were completely wrong. I never stopped wanting you.'

She shook her head. 'It had been obvious for some time that you were bored to death with me.'

'I was no such thing.'

'Why bother to lie? It got so that I scarcely saw you from one week's end to another, and you hardly ever made love to me...'

'I'm only too aware that I neglected you, and I very much regret it, but I had to be away a great deal. I didn't want to be, but circumstances left me no alternative.

'Where I did go badly wrong was in expecting you to cope without giving you the reassurance you needed. But I was under a great deal of stress myself and not really thinking straight when it came to personal matters.

'I ought to have realized how you felt—talked to you more, made you understand—instead of shutting you out.'

Caris's pansy-blue eyes were sad when she said, 'You hardly talked to me at all; you never had time. When you weren't actually away you were always busy at the office or in some meeting.

'If I needed you for any reason I could never get hold of you. You were hardly ever home; on the very few occasions you were, you were distant, preoccupied.'

'I told you why.'

'You told me hardly anything, and what you did tell me sounded very much as though you were just trying to make excuses.'

'I never made any excuses I told you the simple truth—that my father was ill, and I was up to my neck in work.'

Impatient now, she brushed aside his words. 'Though at first I tried hard not to believe it, I knew in my heart of hearts that you'd grown tired of me and found another woman.'

'I'd done nothing of the kind,' he stated categorically.

'There *was* no other woman. There never *has* been since met you.'

'There's really no point in denying it.' With quiet certainty she went on, 'I happened to see you with her one lunchtime

Watching him frown, she continued, 'I'd been having lunc at the Dorset with a client and we were just on the point c leaving when I caught sight of you in the foyer. There wa a woman with you. You had an arm around her and yo were standing close together deep in conversation. Ther was something about the pair of you, a kind of *intimacy* tha made it plain you were more than just friends.'

'What was this mystery woman like?'

'Tall, blonde, very nice looking, smartly dressed... I sav her kiss you, so don't tell me you can't remember her.'

His face cleared. 'As a matter of fact I remember her ver well and, yes, she kissed my cheek.'

Caris was hurrying on, 'You didn't come home that nigh I presume you were with her?'

'Yes, I was with her,' he admitted. 'That is, until she lef to catch a late plane back to Boston to join her husband.'

'Her husband?'

'Matthew was part of some delegation or other and the were going on to San Francisco the following day, so Isobe had seized the chance to make a flying visit to Albany to se her father... Who happened to be my father too.'

Feeling hollow inside, Caris said, 'You mean it was you sister?'

'You must have heard me talk about Bel? You and she ha never met because she and her husband—an ardent politi cian—lived in Washington and were always rushing off some where on some campaign or other. If I had got back home tha night I would probably have mentioned seeing her.'

'But you didn't.'

'No, I was with my father. He'd had a stroke the previou

night. That's why Bel came—it was his second. The first had seemed to be a relatively minor one, but the second was a great deal more serious, and he was admitted to a private nursing-home.'

Though she had only met him a couple of times, Caris had liked James Devereux. Shocked now, she said, 'I knew he was ailing, but I never for a moment imagined it was quite that serious. Why didn't you tell me? Why let me go on thinking he just wasn't well?'

'I couldn't see the point of worrying you.'

'You mean you didn't think I'd care?'

'I don't mean anything of the kind. I know you liked my father and he liked you.'

'Then you should have told me!' she cried passionately. 'Instead of shutting me out as though I was a stranger.'

'I didn't mean to shut you out—but you were so over-worked, pushed to the limit by that father of yours, and I didn't want to add to your concerns. After all, there was nothing you could have done.'

Close to tears, she said, 'At least I could have been there for you.'

She saw by his face that that cry from the heart had touched a chord. 'I'm sorry,' he said quietly. 'I see now how wrong I was. I guess I just wasn't used to handling a relationship like ours. I've always been a rather private person where my deepest emotions were concerned. I've tended to keep them to myself, and old habits die hard.

'My father once admitted that emotionally he'd been a loner too. That is, until he met my mother and she taught him how to loosen up and share his innermost feelings, how to lean on her as she leaned on him.'

Regretfully he added, 'The one thing she never managed to teach him was how to stop being a workaholic, how to relax and delegate. He devoted all his adult working life to

Devereux Hotels and was only satisfied when he had a firm grip on the reins.

'After my mother died, he drove himself even harder, trying to run the company single-handed, working all hours when problems arose, barely stopping to eat. That burden of work and worry was too much for any one man, and I firmly believe that the stress helped to make him ill.

'After his second stroke I had no choice but to shoulder the lot, at least until I could find one or two good men to help me run things. So, what with the workload and the need to visit my father, I had very little time. When he became critically ill and seemed in danger of slipping away, I very often stayed the night.'

She moistened dry lips. Feeling a tightness in her chest, she asked, 'What happened to him?'

'He died a short time after you left.'

'I'm so sorry,' she whispered. 'I just wish you'd told me how bad things really were.'

'In retrospect, I wish I had. But because of the Devereux company rules I wasn't at liberty to divulge just how ill he was. I was even forced to warn Bel not to talk about it. If the news that he was at death's door had got out, it would have made the Devereux share prices drop dramatically and caused widespread panic-selling—which was the last thing the company wanted.

'You see, after his first stroke my father had made several serious errors of judgement. Errors, we discovered too late, that had provided Emorna—a rival hotel chain who for some time had been trying to buy us out—with just the opportunity they'd been hoping for.

'In consequence they'd been secretly buying up shares in Devereux Hotels and were just waiting their chance to make a hostile takeover.

'I intended to tell you everything the minute the attempted takeover had been defeated...'

With a sigh, he went on, 'If only you'd stayed to thrash things out rather than running as soon as my back was turned. Why did you do it, Caris? I thought you loved me.'

'I *did* love you.'

'But you didn't trust me.'

She couldn't deny his charge, and she felt shocked and ashamed that he had had to shoulder such a burden of work and worry on his own while she had believed the worst of him.

'Was that why you left as you did?'

Remembering her own despair, her humiliation, the feeling that her pride and self-respect had been trampled into the mud yet again, she said unsteadily, 'I suppose it was, in a way.'

'Did you do it especially to hurt me?'

She shook her head. 'I thought you would probably be relieved if I went.'

'Relieved! When I got home that night and found you were gone, I almost went out of my mind. Oh Caris, how could we have made such a mess of things?'

'I don't know.' Then she went on bleakly, 'Yes, I do. There was no real closeness—we didn't talk to one another, didn't communicate—and there was lack of trust on both sides.'

At his quick glance, she pointed out, 'You didn't trust me enough to tell me about your father's illness and all your business worries.'

Before he could refute that, she added, 'And your attitude, the way you distanced yourself, made me believe you didn't care.'

'I cared much more than you'll ever know.'

She felt suddenly devastated. If that was true, how could she have got things so wrong?

For the first time she wondered whether her failure to trust him been fuelled by old insecurities.

Why, after everything they'd shared, had it been so easy to believe that he had found another woman, that he no longer loved her?

Was it because, subconsciously, she had always thought of him as a rich, aristocratic playboy, charming and fickle just like Karl? Without being fully aware of it, had she *expected* him to tire of her in the same way Karl had done?

Feeling as if she had left a plane at thirty-thousand feet without a parachute, she realized that on some level she *had* always feared it would end that way, had almost been waiting for it to happen.

That realization was immediately followed by another that was equally disturbing: if he really *hadn't* cared, surely he would have just let her go without another thought?

He wouldn't have spent three years looking for her and, having finally found her, wouldn't have taken the trouble to lie about his feelings.

But regardless of what his feelings had once been their relationship was over and done with, a thing of the past. They had made too many mistakes, killed what had been between them. There was no going back.

And he must have known that.

So why had he spent so much time and money looking for her?

He had said he wanted answers to his questions—peace of mind. Yet he hadn't asked the one question she had expected him to ask—the question she had feared the most.

CHAPTER NINE

FEELING emotionally exhausted, totally drained, Caris leaned her head against the back of the chair and stared into the fire.

Watching her face, recognizing that exhaustion, Zander lapsed into silence. There was plenty of time to learn what he still needed to know.

Wind and rain continued to beat relentlessly against the mullioned windows, while thunder tore the sky apart and flashes of lightning lit up the ever-deepening gloom.

But in spite of the noise of the storm raging outside the flickering firelight had a soothing effect, and the tension gradually began to ease.

She was half asleep when Zander rose and tossed some more logs onto the stove, remarking as he did so, 'Time's getting on...'

Time's getting on... The ominous words rang in her ears. Soon it would be night, and then what?

As she struggled to keep the sudden panic under control, he went on prosaically, 'Which means it's time I was digging out some candles.'

'But surely we could go now?' she burst out. 'There's no further reason to stay.'

The faint hope that he might agree to leave died as he said positively, 'There are several reasons—one being that our clothes are still wet.'

Afraid to ask what the others were, she bit her lip and lapsed into silence

Looking through the cupboards, he located a variety of old candlesticks and a supply of tall wax candles. Having lit half a dozen, he placed them round the room then drew the curtains against the coming night. He asked, 'You must be getting hungry?'

All the emotional stress had taken away her appetite, and she was about to say she wasn't, when she thought better of it.

At least getting ready a meal of some kind would occupy him, keep his mind on the present.

Her voice as level as she could manage, she agreed, 'A little.'

After a look through the store cupboard, he reported, 'Though the menu is necessarily limited, you have a choice of canned soup, beef casserole, macaroni cheese, or spaghetti in a cream and white-wine sauce.'

'I don't mind in the slightest,' she told him. 'Whatever you fancy.'

After her previous night's disturbed sleep, Caris found the warmth of the fire soporific, and while Zander set about preparing the meal she rested her head against the back of the chair, tired both physically and mentally.

She was gazing drowsily into the fire when Zander's hand softly stroked her cheek. She smiled dreamily and turned her face up to his, giving a sigh of pleasure as his mouth brushed hers.

Her lips parted beneath the light pressure of his, and when he deepened the kiss her arms went around his neck and, her whole body melting, she kissed him back.

Then, suddenly scared by her own reaction to that kiss, she drew back, demanding raggedly, 'Why did you do that?'

'Because your meal's ready.' Bringing her food on a small

ound tray, he set it down on the coffee table. 'I thought we'd
have it on our laps.'

Taking her confusion out on him, she ordered sharply, 'You
had no right to kiss me—don't ever do it again. I hated it!'

As soon as the words were out, she knew she'd made a bad
mistake.

She sat still as a statue. His hands moved to cup her chin
and tilt her head back, so that she found herself looking up
into his handsome face, intriguingly inverted.

'So tell me,' he said silkily. 'If my kiss is such anathema
to you, why did you kiss me back?'

'I didn't,' she denied hoarsely. 'I've already made it clear
I can't stand you touching me.'

Quietly furious, he said, 'Well, that's too bad.'

His hands released their hold, but almost before she realized it he had moved round the chair and, taking her shoulders, pulled her to her feet and into his arms.

Her initial protest was stifled as his mouth closed over
hers. It was a hard kiss, meant to relieve some of the anger
that was simmering just beneath the surface.

If that was all it had been she might have found the will
to resist, but after a second or two it metamorphosed into a
lover's kiss.

It held an urgency, a passionate hunger, that swept her
away. With no further thought of resisting, her lips parted to
allow that sweet invasion.

Within seconds her head was swimming and her very soul
had lost its way.

When finally he let her go, dazed and shaken to the core,
she sank limply back into her chair while, apparently unmoved, he fetched his own food and sat down opposite as if
nothing had happened.

When she made no attempt to pick up the tray, he enquired,
'Can you reach it all right?'

She looked at the bowl of spaghetti, never having felt less like eating. She said unsteadily, 'I really don't want anything to eat.'

He glanced at her with a frown. 'A short while ago you said you did.'

She shook her head. 'I've changed my mind.'

'Don't be a fool,' he urged. 'There's no point in starving yourself.'

'I really couldn't manage it.'

Putting his own food aside, he got to his feet and, setting her tray on her lap, cajoled, 'Try.'

After a moment, without the energy to fight, she picked up her fork.

When she had taken the first mouthful he resumed his seat and began to eat his own.

Much to her surprise, once she had started on the pasta she found her normal healthy appetite had returned and, in spite of everything, she was able to empty the bowl.

When the simple meal was over, without a word Zander cleared away and made a fresh pot of coffee, handing Caris a cup.

While she sipped it, she stared into the flames and wondered helplessly where all this was going to end. Zander's kiss and her own response to it had shaken her, and her clumsy attempt to deny that response had angered him and brought a reprisal that had shaken her even more.

But after a kiss that had rocked her world he had walked away, unmoved.

Apparently unmoved. But then he had always been more adept than she at hiding his feelings.

Glancing up at him now through a fan of thick, dark lashes, she found his eyes were fixed on her and she looked hastily away.

But even that fleeting glance couldn't help but register

the look on his face—a look of passionate desire. A look she knew well. A look that stopped her breath and made her heart start to race impossibly fast.

A split second later it had vanished as though it had never been, while the flickering firelight played across his features, casting shadows in the hollows and highlighting the planes.

Forcing herself to breathe, to remain outwardly calm, she tried to tell herself that she'd been mistaken, that it had simply been a trick of the light. But she knew it hadn't, and her stomach tied itself in knots.

Though he no longer loved her—perhaps he even hated her—that look had made it abundantly clear that he still wanted her physically.

She shivered. Though Zander had more self-control than most men, anger could fuel passion—as she had already discovered—and the knowledge made her feel even more vulnerable.

When he moved suddenly, she jumped. But with scarcely a glance in her direction he set about filling a large kettle with water and setting it on the stove to heat.

Realizing with a sinking heart that he was making preparations for bedtime, she bit her lip.

Resuming his seat, he assured her, 'There's no need to look quite so alarmed. Though we'll have to share the bed, it's plenty large enough.'

With panic in her voice, she said, 'I don't want to share a bed.'

'We've done it before.'

'I can't bear the thought of lying next to you.'

'From your reaction when I kissed you earlier, I know that's not true. Your response was all I could have asked for.'

'When you kissed me, just for a minute it took me back to when—' Breaking off abruptly, she swallowed before going on. 'But I meant what I said.'

'I believe you *want* to mean it, but that's not the same thing.

'I *do* mean it,' she insisted.

Hearing the panic in her voice, he said, 'Don't worry, wouldn't dream of trying to force you. In fact, I promise no to lay a finger on you unless you want me to. If you come to me it has to be willingly, eagerly, as you once did.'

'I'll never do that.'

'You said you loved me.'

'I did. But now it's dead. All in the past.'

'Real love doesn't die that easily.'

Somehow she forced herself to say, 'In that case it couldn't have been real. It must have been just infatuation.'

His jaw tightened as though she'd struck him. Then he shrugged his shoulders. 'Well, even if you don't love me, you still want me and you'll come to me because you can't help yourself.'

'I *don't* still want you, and I *can* help myself.'

Smiling a little, he said with conviction, 'Forgive me, but I don't believe you.'

Desperate to shake that certainty, she snatched a familiar name out of the air and said, 'You should. I could never let Nathan down.'

'Who's Nathan?'

'My boyfriend.'

She saw him stiffen before he said, 'This is the first I've heard about a boyfriend. Why haven't you mentioned him before?'

'Because my private life is none of your business.'

He looked at her through narrowed green eyes. 'You'd better tell me about him. That is, if he actually exists?'

On slightly firmer ground now, she said, 'Of course he exists.'

Nathan was a nice-looking thirty-eight-year-old widower

she had met in the course of her work. He had asked her out quite a few times, and his kisses had been pleasant.

But no more than that. He had never once caused her heart to miss a beat, never once made her feel delightfully confused and breathless, never once raised her temperature by a single degree—so that, when he had tried to take things further, it had been only too easy to say no.

Then the company he worked for had relocated him to Wales and, her heart intact, untouched, she had waved him goodbye without any regrets.

'So what's his surname? What does he do? Why weren't you meeting him on a Saturday night?'

'His name's Nathan Thomas. He works for an insurance company. And I wasn't meeting him tonight because at the moment he's in Wales.'

'And I suppose you're missing him desperately?' Zander asked mockingly.

'How did you guess?'

'Has he been your boyfriend long?'

Deciding on a gamble, she said, 'He's rather more than just a boyfriend.'

Zander's gaze sharpened. 'How much more?'

'We're engaged to be married.'

The mockery vanished entirely and for an instant shock took its place. Then, his face wiped clear of all expression, he leaned forward and lifted her bare left hand. 'You're not wearing a ring.'

'No, but we'll be going to choose one as soon as he gets back.'

Zander ran long, lean fingers over his chin, assessing the truth of her words, before asking, 'So when did he propose, exactly?'

'Just before he went.'

'And you said yes?'

'Of course.'

He jumped to his feet and paced like a caged lion for a moment or two before standing over her and demanding, 'Why did you agree to marry him?'

'Because I...I love him.'

'You don't sound terribly sure.'

'I'm quite sure,' she insisted, then spoiled it all by adding, 'I'm *extremely* fond of him.'

'Fond!'

'There's no need to sneer,' she said sharply. 'It may seem tame to you, but genuine fondness can outlast a mistaken passion.'

He let that go but, seeing a white line appear round his mouth, she added for good measure, 'And I'm sure he'll make a good husband.'

His face set and hard, Zander demanded, 'What about a lover?'

'Yes... Yes, of course.'

'Have you slept together?'

'That's none of your business.'

'Have you?' he demanded savagely.

'I've no intention of telling you.'

'I don't believe you have.'

'Believe what you want.'

Zander's short, sharp sigh was audible as he returned to his chair.

There was silence for a while, then out of the blue he asked, 'So what made you decide to be an estate agent?'

The abrupt change of topic, though a surprise, was a welcome one; she answered, 'I never wanted to be a lawyer. I'd only trained to please my father. So, when I came to England, instead of looking for work with a law firm I chose to join Aunt Jo in the agency. When she died and left everything to me, I decided to have a go at running it myself.'

'I see. And now you're a thriving estate agent and about to get engaged to the man of your dreams.'

Caris ignored the sarcasm. As the silence closed in once more, she tried to bolster herself with the thought that if he believed she was going to marry another man he would back off. And once they had left Gracedieu they would never have to meet again. Their lives and futures would be totally separate. He would go back to the States and she would...

What would she do?

Live the rest of her days alone, unloved and lonely, with no partner and no family.

It was a bleak prospect.

If he had never come back into her life, she might have eventually succeeded in burying the past and convinced herself that her feelings for him had been ephemeral. But, now she knew beyond a shadow of a doubt that he still affected her as much as ever, how could she even contemplate loving another man?

She sighed. It had been a long, emotionally exhausting day. Her brain felt muddled, her eyes were heavy and waves of tiredness were starting to wash over her.

Seeing her heavy lids begin to droop, Zander remarked, 'You look shattered, so I suggest we get some sleep. There are plenty of pillows and clean bedclothes in the cupboards, so I'll make the bed up while you have first turn in the bathroom.'

He rose and, having produced a couple of fresh towels, handed her one before picking up the kettle.

'I noticed there were some unopened packs of toiletries in the cabinet,' he went on. 'And there's just about enough hot water to wash in, so all you need now is a candle to light your way...'

As Caris left the glowing warmth of the fire and followed him to the bathroom in the flickering candlelight, the floor cold beneath her bare feet, she once again felt that strong sense of déjà vu.

Only this wasn't a mistaken feeling that the same little scene was being played over again. It was so similar to what had happened at Owl Lodge that it was really like history repeating itself, and she found the whole concept extremely disturbing.

Having set the candle down on a convenient shelf and put the kettle on a stool by the sink, Zander left at once, closing the door behind him.

Cold, dank air wrapped her in a clammy shroud. The candle cast grotesque, elongated shadows and her reflection in the mirror put her in mind of a Hallowe'en mask.

Striving to calm her agitation, she looked in the bathroom cabinet. Amongst its contents were several tablets of soap, an unopened tube of toothpaste and a pack of cellophane-wrapped toothbrushes.

She helped herself to a yellow one and, like some automaton, began to prepare for the night ahead.

A night she was dreading.

Zander had said he wouldn't try to force her and she believed him. But if he kissed her, touched her, even looked at her in a certain way, her whole body came to life.

It had been that way from the start. He had stolen her heart at their very first meeting, stopped her breath and, like dropping a lighted match into dry straw, sent her up in flames.

She had wanted to be in his arms, his bed, loved and wanted him as she had loved and wanted no other man. But after all that had happened there was no going back.

Shivering, she finished cleaning her teeth and washed as quickly as possible before huddling into her robe once more and brushing and loosely braiding her long, dark hair.

Picking up the candle, she made her way back through the gloom. In spite of all her concerns it was a relief to leave the cold dankness of the bathroom for the cosy warmth of the kitchen.

Zander was putting the finishing touches to the bed, a lock of fair hair falling over his forehead and his robe gaping a little to expose the strong column of his throat and an expanse of broad chest.

He glanced up, and at the sight of her shiny face and plait his own face softened. She thought he was about to make some teasing remark, but in the end he only asked casually, 'All finished?'

She nodded and, looking anywhere but at him, mumbled, 'I've left you half the hot water.'

She hadn't intended to repeat the pattern but hadn't been able to help herself.

The look on his face spoke volumes, but all he said was, 'In that case, I'll go and take advantage of your generosity.'

When he had relieved her of the candle and departed, she let her glance stray to the bed, which he had pulled closer to the fire.

It looked both comfortable and inviting. But a double bed was much too emotive. Every nerve in her body tightened; she looked hastily away and, keeping her gaze averted, took her seat by the fire.

Her previous tiredness had vanished and she was tense and on-edge. Unable to relax, she tried to steel herself for what lay ahead.

Though she had been waiting for him, she jumped convulsively when he returned.

'Sorry,' he said apologetically. 'Did I startle you?' As she shook her head he went on, 'I thought if you were half-asleep I might have done.'

'I wasn't half-asleep. In fact, I don't feel tired any longer.'

'Well, if you're in no hurry to go to bed, how would you like a nightcap? Say, a small brandy?'

'Brandy? Is there any?'

'I found a bottle in one of the cupboards—no doubt kept for medicinal purposes.'

Wondering if it would be wise, she hesitated.

As though reading her thoughts, he assured her sardonically, 'There's no need to worry; I'm not planning to get you drunk so I can have my evil way with you.'

Needing something to steady her, she said, 'In that case, I will have a drop please.'

Producing a bottle of Cognac, he remarked, 'I'm afraid I can only find tumblers.'

'That's fine by me.' She was pleased with her casual tone.

When the brandy was poured he passed her one of the tumblers and sat down opposite. For a while they sipped in silence, watching the fire. Then, indicating her empty glass, Zander enquired, 'Another drop?'

The brandy had had a beneficial effect and, feeling more confident, she said, 'Do you know, I think I might.'

He poured another measure and handed her back the glass; whether by accident or design his fingers brushed hers and the tumbler jerked in her hand so that she banged it down clumsily.

'Dear me,' he murmured mildly. 'You *are* jumpy.'

Completely thrown because she had thought herself steadier she indicated the shadowy room and the bed, crying, 'Surely you don't expect me to be at ease in this situation?'

Deliberately misunderstanding her, he said, 'It isn't all that different from Owl Lodge, and you were happy there.'

Stung, she cried, 'That was different! You weren't angry, bitter and resentful then.'

'I had no reason to be. I had no suspicion then that you were going to turn my life upside down by walking out on me.'

But that was unjust, she thought. In the end it was *he*

who had screwed up *her* life. *He* who had thought and said the unforgivable…

Iron bands tightening round her heart, she whispered, 'If only you hadn't come into my office that day—'

She broke off as he rose to face her. His face a white, taut mask, he demanded, 'Is that all you care? Do you *really* wish we'd never met?'

She tried to say yes, but was unable to; completely overwrought now, she burst into tears.

'Oh, hell! I'm sorry.' Pulling her into his arms, he cradled her dark head against his chest.

Struggling to quell the sobs that kept rising in her throat, she heard the anguish in his voice as he repeated, 'I'm sorry, I'm sorry… Don't cry, my love, please don't cry…'

She could feel the warmth of his skin and his heart thundering beneath her cheek; could smell the clean male scent of him. Suddenly, as if the intervening years had never been, everything she had once felt for him came flooding back like a tidal wave.

When he lifted her face to kiss away the tears she clung to him, and when he kissed her mouth she kissed him back with all the love that was filling her heart.

The first faint streaks of dawn were just beginning to filter into the room when she stirred and opened her eyes. The candles had guttered and gone out, and the stove had only a faint red glow beneath its whitish blanket of ash.

The air in the room struck chill, but she felt cosy and warm, and utterly content. Close by her side, Zander was still sleeping peacefully. She could see very little in the gloom but she could hear his light, even breathing.

Her eyelids drifting shut again, she lay half-asleep and half-awake, remembering how harsh and ragged it had been the previous night while he'd been making love to her.

Remembering too how his hunger had seemed insatiable and his kisses had held an urgency, a kind of desperation, that had swept her along and made her feel the same.

She had been his lover in every sense of the word, rendering passion for passion, giving everything she had to give and more. There had been nothing in the universe but the pair of them and what they had felt for each other.

Only later, when some of the urgency had abated, had their love-making become sweeter and more leisurely, tenderness and caring mingling with the passion, at times eclipsing it.

She had been filled with a joy and happiness beyond words, the kind of joy and happiness she hadn't felt for more than three years...

All at once her eyelids flew open and she began to tremble violently.

After all her warnings to herself, what had made her ignore the past and behave so foolishly?

But she knew the answer to that question. Her determination had crumbled into dust when he had called her 'my love'.

But they were just words. She couldn't really believe he still loved her. If by any chance he did have any feelings of affection left for her, they would surely die if he discovered what she was keeping from him?

And he seemed certain to.

Last night, after kissing her, he'd settled her head on his shoulder and said softly, 'The barriers are down now. Tomorrow we'll really talk, lay the last of the ghosts to rest...'

Her blood ran cold. She knew exactly what he meant by 'lay the last of the ghosts to rest'. But if she was forced to bring the whole thing into the open and tell him the truth he would never forgive her.

So what could she do?

The only way to avoid a confrontation she dreaded was to leave now, before he awoke. If she could find his car keys...

With a caution born of fear she slid carefully out of bed and crept across the kitchen to where their clothing was hanging. Her heart in her mouth, she let down the pulley, flinching when it squeaked a little.

None of her clothes were completely dry and everything felt miserably cold and clammy, but she struggled into them as quickly as possible before pulling on her damp shoes.

Then with shaking hands she went through the pockets of his trousers.

They were empty.

His light jacket was hanging over a chair, but again the search proved fruitless.

So where were the keys likely to be?

Creeping back across the living room, she spotted his navy-blue towelling robe lying at the foot of the bed but, having felt in the pockets, once again her hopes were dashed.

She was about to look in the first of the drawers, when Zander stirred in his sleep and began to show signs of waking.

No, it was too risky to go on looking. It would be better to leave now and make her escape on foot. When she reached the road, hopefully she could get a lift fairly quickly, but if not she would walk towards the town until she could.

Pulling on her mac, she grabbed her bag and was moving cautiously towards the door when Zander sighed and threw out an arm.

Her heart thudding against her ribs, she froze, afraid to move a muscle.

After a minute, when there was no further sound or movement, she plucked up courage and, tiptoeing out, closed the door silently behind her and hurried across the hall.

Once outside, in the grey bleakness of an early dawn she found it was cold and wet underfoot but no longer raining.

The sight of Zander's car jolted her and made her realize

that if she went down the drive and he awoke and came after her he could easily overtake her before she reached the road.

But surely he wouldn't come after her?

Or would he? She couldn't be certain.

The eight-foot-high wall surrounding this part of the park meant she had to use the gates. But rather than keep to the drive itself, it would be safer to take a parallel route. That way, she would be screened by the bushes and rhododendrons, and would only need to join the drive just before she reached the Lodge.

Leaving the house behind her, she set off over the undulating parkland as fast as possible. The rough, grassy terrain scattered with snapped twigs and broken branches wasn't easy to negotiate, but in spite of that she made quite good time.

Though straining her ears, she heard no sound of a car and, knowing she could only be a few hundred yards from the lodge, she was breathing a sigh of relief when, topping a rise, she got a nasty shock.

Ahead where the ground dipped into a hollow both the drive and the surrounding countryside had disappeared beneath a brown lake of water.

As she gazed blankly at the scene before her, she realized that, after so much heavy rain, on its lower reaches—where two fast-flowing streams joined it—the River Darley must have burst its banks.

If that was the case, the lie of the land made it almost certain that by road at least Gracedieu would be cut off from the outside world until the flood subsided.

So where did that leave her?

After a moment's thought she realized that her best bet was to go cross-country and head for the small village of Hallfield. The pub there—the Hallfield Arms—was run by a pleasant middle-aged couple who would almost certainly let her use their phone to call a taxi.

Hopefully, the upper reaches of the river would be free from flooding, and she knew from past hikes that she could get to Hallfield either by crossing the Old Mill bridges, or going another quarter of a mile or so to Darley Bridge.

Her spirits rising a little, she turned and headed across the park.

CHAPTER TEN

THE sky was growing appreciably lighter now, which made things easier, and in a little over fifteen minutes she was approaching the picturesque cluster of estate cottages.

The small hamlet—at one time a tight-knit community complete with a small chapel and a pub—had been deserted, unlived-in for years, and was in danger of going to rack and ruin if it wasn't rescued soon.

Until then she had tried not to think about Zander, but now she found herself wondering what he was doing, what his reaction had been when he had discovered that she'd gone.

Trying to push his image out of her mind, she skirted an overgrown patch of ground that had once been the central green and dropped down to a track that ran alongside the river, swollen now and carrying with it a load of debris.

She soon found the going was treacherous, wet and slippery with mud, with an obstacle course of deep puddles that meant she had to pick her way with the greatest care.

Hurrying had caused a painful stitch in her left side that over the last half-mile had grown worse, but she bolstered herself with the thought that she couldn't have too far to go.

Then, turning a bend, she saw that she had reached her goal. A little way ahead, where a woodland trail that ran back in the direction of the manor joined the track, the river divided, forming a narrow island with a humpbacked stone bridge on either side to connect it to the outer banks.

The Old Mill stood on the island. Once a thriving concern, it had supplied the entire estate with flour produced from crops grown on the nearby farms. It pre-dated the cottages by more than a century and had been semi-derelict for years.

Part of the upper storey had been built out above the millrace, and the wooden structure sagged precariously over the water, its once sturdy timbers splintered and broken.

The huge waterwheel—its rotting paddles covered with green slime—was being pounded and smashed by the surging water, which triumphantly carried away its spoils.

Crossing the river at that point was a daunting prospect. A raging torrent of water carrying a mass of debris and tree branches, was thundering downstream, battering the foundations of the mill and the crumbling stone of the bridges.

Going on up to Darley Bridge would add quite a bit to her journey, but, looking at the tumultuous scene before her, she decided it would be preferable.

She had walked some distance when she saw that up ahead, where the river formed a low-lying S bend, it had breached its banks. The track and the approaches to the bridge itself had disappeared, and brown, swirling water stretched for as far as she could see.

Trying not to panic, she faced the fact that if she wanted to get to Hallfield her only option was to cross the river at the Old Mill.

As quickly as she could, she retraced her steps. When she approached the mill once again the noise became deafening but, whipping up her courage, she was just about to cross the first of the cobbled bridges when a movement caught her eye, different from that of the rushing water.

A tall, bare-headed figure had just emerged from the

woodland trail and was striding up the track in her direc
tion, cutting off any possible retreat.

Her heart racing, and galvanized into action, she hastene
over the bridge and glanced back. He didn't appear to hav
seen her, but she could hardly expect to get across the secon
bridge without attracting his attention.

A moment's thought convinced her that her best optio
was to stay out of sight until he discovered it wasn't possibl
to go on and turned back.

But where could she hide?

The island, cropped by the local sheep, was covered wit
short, scrubby grass and offered no chance of concealmen
The only place she could hide was the mill itself.

Up close, she could see that the derelict building leane
drunkenly and the huge, half-open door hung loosely on it
hinges.

Venturing inside, she found it was a complete shambles
Some of the flooring had broken away, leaving a jagged hol
through which she could see the brown water rushing past
and part of one wall had collapsed, causing the upper sto
rey to sag dangerously and the heavy machinery to lean at
crazy angle.

The entire structure seemed to creak and groan and shud
der from the buffeting it was receiving, and she could hea
nothing beyond that and the surging water.

It was the change in the light coming through the doo
that alerted her, even before she heard Zander's voice call
ing, 'Caris, Caris… Are you in there?'

She stood quite still, hardly daring to breathe.

He called again. Terrified that he was going to come inside
heart pounding, she fled across the rough wooden floorboard
and began to climb the stairs to the upper storey where sh
would be safely out of sight.

She had almost reached the top when the whole place

emed to lurch and, suddenly afraid, she turned to go back
hen there was a wrenching, splintering noise and a large
ction of the upper storey came crashing down.

Though the wooden stairs shook badly they remained in-
act; shocked, she clung on to the hand rail until the worst of
e noise had died away, leaving only the creaks and groans
f the timbers settling.

Then she had an even worse shock. Looking through the
wirling dust and particles of debris to the devastation below,
he saw Zander lying ominously still, pinned beneath a huge
ooden beam.

For an instant she stood frozen with horror, then she turned
nd stumbled back down the stairs.

The impact of the heavy timbers had caused the lower floor
tilt so acutely that she was forced to crawl on her hands
nd knees over the broken boards, which creaked and gave
armingly even under her slight weight.

When she reached his side she saw that his eyes were
losed and blood was trickling down his face from a wound
bove his left temple.

Oh, please God, don't let him be dead, she prayed silently,
esperately.

When she checked, her heart in her mouth, she found that
e was breathing and his heartbeat seemed steady, and gave
hanks.

She cleared away the lighter debris that had fallen on him.
hen, hoping against hope that nothing was broken, she strug-
led to move the heavy beam that lay across his thighs.

She might as well have tried to move a mountain.

But somehow she had to get him out of there before the
est of the rotten timbers gave way, plunging everything into
he millrace.

She drew a deep, shuddering breath then, stroking his
heek, said urgently, 'Zander?'

He opened dazed eyes. At the sight of her, his face lit up. Then he groaned. 'I was hoping you weren't in here after all.' He spoke with difficulty, his words halting and slurred.

Her voice as steady as she could make it, she asked, 'What shall I do?'

'Get out!' When she made no move to obey he said, 'Go on, damn you—*now*—before the whole lot gives way.'

She shook her head.

'Go on, go!' he urged.

'I'm not leaving you.'

Pushing himself up groggily, he struggled to move the beam, but the lower end was jammed against one of the broken joists, and even though she added her strength it refused to budge.

When he fell back exhausted, she lifted his fair head into her lap and wiped the blood and sweat from his face with her skirt.

'For God's sake don't be a fool, Caris,' he groaned. 'Get out while you can.'

'Not without you.'

He was silent for a moment or two then, his voice barely audible, he whispered, 'I love you.'

Her tears falling on his face, she answered, 'I love you too.'

His eyes were closed and she thought he had drifted back into unconsciousness when he begged hoarsely, 'Please go. You can't do any good by staying. It would take a miracle.'

'Then I'll pray for one.'

At the same moment there was a violent impact and a section of the steeply sloping floor, including the joist that held the beam, broke away and fell into the rushing water.

Deprived of its support, the heavy beam slid after it; and though once again her prayers had been answered, Zander

was free. A split second later a further section fell and a pile
of debris followed, threatening to carry him with it.

Bracing herself, Caris clung to him with all her strength
until the upheaval had subsided. Then, sobbing with relief,
she urged him to sit up and start to crawl to safety.

Their progress seemed agonizingly slow, but eventually
they made it through the door and onto firm ground.

Once outside, though he seemed only semi-conscious, he
managed to stagger across the bridge before his legs buckled
under him.

It had started to pour with rain once more and, crouching
in the wet beside him, she covered him as best she could with
her mac.

His eyes were closed and she saw that his face was ashen.
It could be shock setting in, she realized anxiously, or con-
cussion.

Whichever, he needed to be out of this rain and under cover
as soon as possible.

She shook him a little. 'If you tell me where your car keys
are…'

He didn't answer, and she was about to shake him again
when his eyes opened once more. His voice halting, barely
audible, he said, 'My car's close by, at the end of a woodland
trail… The keys are in the ignition…'

Giving thanks, she ran, calling over her shoulder, 'Don't
go to sleep.'

It was only a minute or two's work to fetch the car and
turn it round. Then came the task of getting him into it.

Eventually, though extremely groggy, he managed with her
help to struggle to his feet and climb into the passenger seat.

As soon as he was safely buckled in, she rejoined the trail
and drove back to the house as swiftly as possible.

When she had parked as close to the main door as she
could get, he fumbled in his pocket and produced the keys.

Having unlocked the door, she helped him into the hou
and through to the kitchen. The stove, though burning lo
was still throwing out a fair amount of heat and once he w
seated in front of it she tossed on more logs. Bewailing t
lack of a hot shower, she found a towel.

Slowly, fumbling a little, he struggled to strip off and sta
to dry himself.

Shocked by the extensive bruising that had started
appear on his legs and body, she said, 'You ought to have
doctor. But because of the flooding I don't think one cou
get through.'

'I don't need a doctor. I'm very lucky there's nothing br
ken,' he said, his voice slurred.

Forced to agree with that, she helped him into his robe a
onto the bed before going in search of the pads he had us
to clean her grazes.

Having discovered a well-equipped first-aid box in t
same drawer, she returned with a sterile dressing, a roll
adhesive tape, some cotton-wool pads, a small pair of sci
sors and a bottle of tincture of arnica for his bruises.

He seemed barely conscious and his face was still ashe
but whatever had hit him must have struck just a glanci
blow, because to her very great relief the wound above his l
temple, though still bleeding, appeared to be fairly superficia

By the time she had cleaned it and taped a dressing in
place, his eyes were starting to close. But in case the concu
sion proved to be bad and she had to call the air ambulan
she shook him and said quickly, 'Before you go to sleep
need to know where your mobile is.'

'My jacket pocket.'

She found it, along with his wallet and some keys.

Once she had checked that the battery still had power, s
took off her wet things and changed into her robe before si
ting down on the edge of the bed to treat his bruises.

That done to her satisfaction, she drew a chair closer to the bed and sat down to watch him.

After a while some of her anxiety eased when his colour began to improve and he fell into a more natural sleep. She felt for his heartbeat, and was further reassured to find that it seemed to be strong and steady.

When Zander showed signs of waking after sleeping for several hours, and hoping that he would be able to eat, she tipped a couple of tins of beef casserole into a pan and set it on the stove to heat.

She was just putting bowls to warm when, waking suddenly, he sat up, calling, 'Caris... Caris...'

'Yes, yes, I'm here... What is it?'

He drew an unsteady hand over his eyes. 'I thought you'd gone.'

'No, I haven't gone.'

'Are you all right?' he asked urgently. 'You're not hurt in any way?'

'No, I'm quite all right.'

Apparently reassured by her calm reply, he gave a sigh of relief.

'How do *you* feel?' she asked.

'Apart from some stiffness, I feel fine.'

Once again she gave silent thanks before asking, 'Are you hungry? I know I am.'

'Yes, I could certainly eat.'

Spooning the casserole into two bowls, she turned to ask, 'Do you want to stay in bed to eat it?'

But he was already on his feet and making his way to a chair.

She passed him his meal and, taking her own, sat down opposite.

They ate in silence, though the air was charged with emotion and full of things waiting to be said.

Zander scarcely took his eyes off her face, but not until she had cleared away and poured some coffee did he ask, 'Why did you run away again? I thought you wanted our love-making as much as I did.'

'I did,' she said, scarcely above a whisper.

'Then why did you go?'

Her heart was like lead. When she said nothing, he urged, 'Why, Caris? Was it because you really *do* intend to marry another man?'

'No, it wasn't.'

Relief in his voice, he asked, 'Am I to take it this Nathan Thomas doesn't exist?'

'Oh yes, he exists, though I've no intention of marrying him.'

'But he asked you?'

She shook her head. 'It never got that far. I knew from the start that he wasn't the man for me, and since the firm he worked for relocated him to Wales we haven't even been in touch.'

'I see. You just made up that story to help keep me at bay?'

Her silence was answer enough.

'Tell me, Caris, in the three years since you left me *has* there been anyone else?'

'No. After one disastrous relationship...' The words tailed off.

He sighed deeply. 'I'm only too aware that I failed you miserably, and I've spent the last three years bitterly regretting it. But I never stopped loving you, and I never so much as *looked* at another woman after I met you.'

Her chest restricted, she said nothing.

'Even if you believed that I'd grown tired of you and found someone else, after everything that had been between us, all we'd meant to each other, surely you could have stayed to talk to me—given me a chance to refute your allegations?'

Sadly he added, 'I've always believed that love and trust should go hand in hand.'

Cut to the quick, she jumped to her feet and cried fiercely, 'You're a fine one to talk! Even if you loved me, as you say, it was quite obvious that you didn't trust me.'

Rising to face her, he demanded, 'How can you even think that?'

'Quite easily. I'll never forget your face that morning when I told you I might be pregnant. You were horrified, and you can't deny it. Oh yes, I know that afterwards you *said* you were pleased, but your face told a different story.'

'I admit that just at that minute your news came as a shock. I presumed you were still taking the pill, and with so much falling apart around me, so much on my plate, the timing seemed all wrong. I thought—'

'I know quite well what you thought,' she broke in raggedly. 'You thought that I'd noticed you were cooling off and was using the classic ploy to try to trap you into marriage.'

He seized her upper arms. 'That's not true! You got upset and jumped to that conclusion. I told you you were quite mistaken.'

She lifted her chin. 'How could I believe you? When I asked what made you think I would do such a thing, you said other women have tried it.'

'So they have. But I never for one instant thought that *you* were that kind of woman.' Releasing his grip on her arms, he asked helplessly, 'If you thought you might be pregnant, why did you just go like you did?'

'As far as I was concerned, being pregnant was all the more reason to go, all the more reason not to stay with a man I was convinced didn't want either me or an unplanned baby.'

'But I *did* want you, and I would have wanted you even more—if that were possible—if you *had* been carrying my child.'

'Was that the reason you looked for me, because you thought I might be pregnant?'

'It was one of the reasons,' he admitted. 'If you had been, I wanted to look after you both. But it wasn't the only reason by a long chalk. I wanted you back, wanted to spend the rest of my life with you.'

Studying her pale face, he went on with a sigh, 'After our quarrel, when I thought things over, I realized that I'd never actually told you in so many words how much I loved you.

'I went home early that night with the firm intention of telling you how I felt and asking you to be my wife—whether you were pregnant or not.'

Feeling as though a giant fist had tightened around her heart, she sank back into her chair.

He sat down too, before going on, 'And that wasn't a sudden decision. I'd been on the point of asking you to marry me when my father had his second stroke and everything erupted into chaos.

'I'd always hoped to have a traditional wedding with a honeymoon and all the trimmings, and I thought you might feel the same way. So I decided to wait until the crisis was over and we had time to be together, to talk and make plans. I didn't really know how you felt about having a family—somehow we'd never got round to discussing it—but then we'd seemed to have all the time in the world...'

Almost too full for words, but feeling compelled to ask, she managed, 'How do *you* feel about children?'

He answered unhesitatingly, 'I like children. If we had got round to discussing the matter, I would have suggested that we had a year or two on our own and then started a family.

'I'd have liked at least two—if possible, a son to carry on the family name and a daughter just like you. So when you said you might be pregnant, after the first shock I was delighted...

His words had such a devastating effect on her that she found difficulty in breathing.

'But I know that you have no child, so I take it you were mistaken.'

This was what she had been dreading, and involuntarily she stiffened. However, 'I take it you were mistaken' had been framed as a statement rather than a question, so perhaps she could get away without having to answer.

But even as the thought went through her mind something about her rigidity gave Zander pause and made him insist, 'You *were* mistaken, weren't you?'

A rush of emotion choked her into silence and she had to struggle to hold back stinging tears.

His face lost colour. 'You *weren't* mistaken?'

'No,' she whispered.

A white line appearing round his mouth, he asked tightly, 'What happened to our baby? You didn't…?'

Horrified, she cried, 'No, no, of course I didn't!' Endeavouring to keep her voice steady, she went on, 'I was just about three months' pregnant and crossing London by tube when someone bumped into me on a busy escalator. I lost my footing, and the subsequent fall brought on a miscarriage.'

'Why didn't you tell me before?' he asked hoarsely.

'I couldn't bear to talk about it. I knew you'd blame me.'

'My love, of course I don't blame you.'

'But I am to blame,' she said jerkily. 'It was my fault. If I'd stayed with you, it would never have happened. I feel so guilty…'

She stopped, her hands clenched into fists, the oval nails biting deep into her soft palms.

He sighed deeply and, taking each fist in turn, straightened the fingers one at a time, kissing each one as he did so. Then, lifting her hands to his lips, he kissed each palm where her nails had left angry purple marks.

'You've absolutely no need to feel guilty.'

His tenderness was her undoing, and the tears overflowed 'But I have. You see—'

He would have stopped her with a finger to her lips. But she shook her head, needing to tell him everything, needing to unburden herself.

'You see, when I discovered I might be pregnant I was still taking the pill and not thinking about children, so I didn' handle it well. In fact, it came as a great shock, and at first I was anything but pleased. It seemed too soon in our relationship. Unsure how you would react, I was worried about telling you...

'Added to that, I dreaded having to break the news to my father. He was so obsessed with me being a success that knew he would be furious. He'd always been very bitter that an unplanned pregnancy had not only put an end my mother' career but had undermined her health so that she had died before she could give him a son.

'So much seemed against my being pregnant, that it took me a little while to come to terms with it, to grow to love and want the baby and start to feel protective towards it. Then the accident happened. I fell and had a miscarriage...' The tears began to fall in earnest, releasing a flood of pent-up tension and emotion.

Gathering her into his arms, Zander held her close. On groan, he said, 'Oh, my heart's darling, and you went through all this alone...'

Sitting down, he pulled her onto his lap and cradled her close, moving his hand up and down her spine in a gesture that was curiously soothing.

When she was all cried out, he tucked a strand of dark silky hair behind her ear and wiped her wet cheeks on a corner of his towelling robe before asking, 'Feeling better now'

Sniffing, she nodded and, afraid of hurting his bruise

tried to get off his lap. But one arm tightened around her, keeping her where she was, and his free hand tilted her chin so he could look into her eyes.

With his voice gentle but determined, he insisted, 'Losing our baby wasn't your fault. You're not to blame in any way; it was a just a tragic accident. Are you listening?'

She nodded.

'And at least it was loved and wanted.'

She gave a tremulous smile. Though she would never forget her loss, she felt a weight lifting from her shoulders now she had told Zander what had happened.

'Now I suggest we both try to put the past behind us and concentrate on the future. It goes without saying that if it hadn't been for you, I wouldn't *have* a future. But before I thank you for saving my life I want to know why you didn't run while the going was good instead of risking your own life.'

'I couldn't leave you. I don't think I could have borne it if anything had happened to you.'

'Did you really say you loved me, or did I just dream it?'

'No, you didn't dream it.'

'Then tell me again.'

'I love you,' she said simply.

The look on his face wrung her heart and brought fresh tears to her eyes before he said, 'I'd despaired of ever hearing you say those words.'

He began to kiss her, tender, passionate kisses sweeter than wine. Between kisses, he murmured, 'You mean the world to me. I love you more than I believed it was possible to love anyone.'

Unbearably moved, she took a deep breath, and to stop herself crying teased plaintively, 'Well, if you love me as much as you say, I do think you might seriously consider buying Gracedieu.'

'I can see why you're a successful estate agent,' he told her drily.

'If by any chance you *did* decide to buy it,' she persisted, 'What would you do with it?'

He pretended to give her question some thought before answering, '*If* I decided to buy it I imagine that the manor itself could be transformed into a top-class hotel, with a helicopter pad and every facility—something like Conroy Castle.'

'What about the cottages?'

'No doubt the cottages could be used as a kind of annex to make additional period accommodation; a lot of people prefer that kind of separate living. While I think that ideally the manor should be a family home, turning the whole thing into a business would at least serve to keep the estate together.

'But we digress. To get back to what I was saying before you distracted me—knowing how much I love you, will you be my wife?'

When she didn't immediately answer—she was too chocked to speak—he went on, 'I won't insult your intelligence by pleading that I can't live without you. But I would much rather live *with* you. You make me happy, and if in the not too distant future we can start a family, then I couldn't ask for more.

'However,' he went on carefully. 'If we're not destined to be that fortunate, then we'll face it together and make other plans.'

Eager to put his mind at rest, she said quickly, 'The doctor who checked me over after my fall assured me there was no permanent damage done. He added that I was young and healthy, and if I wanted I could go on to have a dozen children.'

She heard the relief in his voice as he said, 'That's good

news.' Quizzically, he added, 'I've always fancied fathering a large family.'

As she gave a little gurgle of laughter, he went on solemnly, 'Though I think a dozen may be just a tad excessive. After all, Gracedieu only boasts eight bedrooms...'

Hardly daring to hope, she objected, 'What does Gracedieu have to do with it?'

'I thought you wanted me to consider buying it?'

'I do, but...'

'Then I'll set your mind at rest: I have every intention of doing just that.'

His declaration earned him a joyful kiss, before she asked, 'But you're not buying it to turn it into a hotel?'

He shook his head. 'To live in.'

When she gazed at him speechlessly, he said, 'I thought you loved the place?'

'I do.'

'In that case, consider it your wedding present. And if there turns out to be insufficient bedrooms we can always build a new wing and add some more.'

'But would *you* want to live in it? I mean you already have a home in the States.'

'There's no law that says we can't have a home in the States and another in England and split our time between the two.'

'But you've a company to run.'

'That's true. However, unlike my father I don't try to run it single-handed. I've put good people in the key positions, so all I have to do is keep abreast of what's going on and OK any major decisions that have to be made. Luckily, modern technology means that that can be done from anywhere in the world.'

Overjoyed, she asked, 'But what will you do about Gracedieu's cottages?'

'If they're renovated and brought up to date, they'll be ideal to house the estate workers.'

'What estate workers?'

'I hope to run the place as it should be run—plant organic crops, grow fruit trees, have glasshouses with tomatoes, herbs, salad ingredients et cetera; keep sheep and deer, make the estate pay its way.'

'You're planning to be a country squire?'

'Hardly. I'll find a good estate manager to run things for me. I want time to live my life and enjoy it, time to spend with my wife and children. Happy now?'

'Very happy.'

His arms closed around her and he held her as if he would never let her go.

Pressed to his heart, she whispered, 'I'm only sorry I ever doubted you.'

'In the circumstances, it was quite understandable. Fate seems to have conspired against us.'

She touched her lips to the warm hollow at the base of his throat. 'I don't know why you're so good to me when all I've given you is grief.'

'That isn't all you've given me.'

Raising her head, she kissed his lips, cutting off the denial. 'But I'll try to make it up to you.'

Returning her kiss with interest, he murmured, 'Well, if you *want* to try, I certainly won't stop you.'

Almost fiercely, she said, 'I love you so much.'

'Sure about that?'

'Quite sure. When you're feeling better, I'll try to prove it to you.'

'I'm already feeling better,' he said with alacrity. 'But I'd like to point out that you still haven't said yes to my proposal—and before you take me to bed I want to be certain you intend to make an honest man of me.'

'Oh, I do.'

'That's what I wanted to hear,' he murmured, and kissed her again.

* * * * *

Read on for a sneak preview of Carol Marinelli's
PUTTING ALICE BACK TOGETHER!

Hugh hired bikes!

You know that saying: 'It's like riding a bike, you never forget'?

I'd never learnt in the first place.

I never got past training wheels.

'You've got limited upper-body strength?' He stopped and looked at me.

I had been explaining to him as I wobbled along and tried to stay up that I really had no centre of balance. I mean *really* had no centre of balance. And when we decided, fairly quickly, that a bike ride along the Yarra perhaps, after all, wasn't the best activity (he'd kept insisting I'd be fine once I was on, that you never forget), I threw in too my other disability. I told him about my limited upper-body strength, just in case he took me to an indoor rock-climbing centre next. I'd honestly forgotten he was a doctor, and he seemed worried, like I'd had a mini-stroke in the past or had mild cerebral palsy or something.

'God, Alice, I'm sorry—you should have said. What happened?'

And then I had had to tell him that it was a self-diagnosis. 'Well, I could never get up the ropes at the gym at school.' We were pushing our bikes back. 'I can't blow-dry the back of my hair...' He started laughing.

Not like Lisa who was laughing at me—he was just laughing and so was I. We got a full refund because we'd only been on our bikes ten minutes, but I hadn't failed. If anything, we were getting on better.

And better.

We went to St Kilda to the lovely bitty shops and I found these miniature Russian dolls. They were tiny, made of tin or something, the biggest no bigger than my thumbnail. Every time we opened them, there was another tiny one, and then another, all reds and yellows and greens.

They were divine.

We were facing each other, looking down at the palm of my hand, and our heads touched.

If I put my hand up now, I can feel where our heads touched.

I remember that moment.

I remember it a lot.

Our heads connected for a second and it was alchemic; it was as if our minds kissed hello.

I just have to touch my head, just there at the very spot and I can, whenever I want to, relive that moment.

So many times I do.

'Get them.' Hugh said, and I would have, except that little bit of tin cost more than a hundred dollars and, though that usually wouldn't have stopped me, I wasn't about to have my card declined in front of him.

I put them back.

'Nope.' I gave him a smile. 'Gotta stop the impulse

spending.'

We had lunch.

Out on the pavement and I can't remember what we ate, I just remember being happy. Actually, I can remember: I had Caesar salad because it was the lowest carb thing I could find. We drank water and I *do* remember not giving it a thought.

I was just thirsty.

And happy.

He went to the loo and I chatted to a girl at the next table, just chatted away. Hugh was gone for ages and I was glad I hadn't demanded Dan from the universe, because I would have been worried about how long he was taking.

Do I go on about the universe too much? I don't know, but what I do know is that something *was* looking out for me, helping me to be my best, not to **** this up as I usually do. You see, we walked on the beach, we went for another coffee and by that time it was evening and we went home and he gave me a present.

Those Russian dolls.

I held them in my palm, and it was the nicest thing he could have done for me.

They are absolutely my favourite thing and I've just stopped to look at them now. I've just stopped to take them apart and then put them all back together again and I can still feel the wonder I felt on that day.

He was the only man who had bought something for me, I mean something truly special. Something beautiful, something thoughtful, something just for me.

A sneaky peek at next month...

MODERN™

INTERNATIONAL AFFAIRS, SEDUCTION & PASSION GUARANTEED

My wish list for next month's titles...

In stores from 17th February 2012:

❏ Roccanti's Marriage Revenge – Lynne Graham

❏ Sheikh Without a Heart – Sandra Marton

❏ The Argentinian's Solace – Susan Stephens

❏ Girl on a Diamond Pedestal – Maisey Yates

In stores from 2nd March 2012:

❏ The Devil and Miss Jones – Kate Walker

❏ Savas's Wildcat – Anne McAllister

❏ A Wicked Persuasion – Catherine George

❏ The Theotokis Inheritance – Susanne James

❏ The Ex Who Hired Her – Kate Hardy

Available at WHSmith, Tesco, Asda, Eason, Amazon and Apple

Just can't wait?

MILLS & BOON® Book Club

2 Free Books!

Get your free books now at
www.millsandboon.co.uk/freebookoffer

Or fill in the form below and post it back to us

THE MILLS & BOON® BOOK CLUB™—HERE'S HOW IT WORKS: Accepting your free books places you under no obligation to buy anything. You may keep the books and return the despatch note marked 'Cancel'. If we do not hear from you, about a month later we'll send you 4 brand-new stories from the Modern™ series priced at £3.30* each. There is no extra charge for post and packaging. You may cancel at any time, otherwise we will send you 4 stories a month which you may purchase or return to us—the choice is yours. *Terms and prices subject to change without notice. Offer valid in UK only. Applicants must be 18 or over. Offer expires 31st July 2012. **For full terms and conditions, please go to www.millsandboon.co.uk**

Mrs/Miss/Ms/Mr (please circle)
_____

First Name
_____

Surname
_____

Address
_____

_____

_____ Postcode _____

E-mail
_____

Send this completed page to: Mills & Boon Book Club, Free Book Offer, FREEPOST NAT 10298, Richmond, Surrey, TW9 1BR

Find out more at
www.millsandboon.co.uk/freebookoffer

Visit us Online

0112/P2XEA

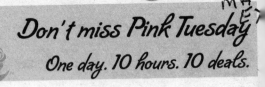

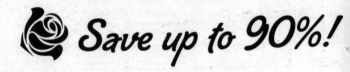